The Shadow Demon

Written by Kenneth Fouts

The Murder

As he steps out from the shadows and approaches his next victim he stops but only

for a moment, he can't help thinking to himself that no one will ever be able to stop

him.   He stands at the end of her bed, he grins a brief smile just slightly revealing

his teeth stained with a dark yellowish tint all while his partly decaying hands where

removing the black hood from his head. His face was pale like the whiteness of the

moon, multiple scars covered his face and in some places chunks of flesh where

missing and showing parts of his skull.   He slowly crept closer and removed the black silk sheet that was covering her naked body, he let yet another smile slip out as he continued to stare at her.

He began to walk up ever so gently and as he did he dragged his index finger up the right side of her body first going from her ankle, then to her thigh, then to the breast until finally he reached her throat.   The creature gently wrapped his fingers around his victims throat and leaned forward, he then began to whisper.

" thiss is what happensss when people medal in my affairsss."

His hand squeezed her throat, 'finally this is it.' he thought.

Just as she woke up her eyes filled with terror.

"no your to late no amount of light can save you now." he said.

As he tightened his grip digging his monstrous claws deep into the sides of her neck and tearing it out, her head fell bouncing off the floor and rolling slightly under the bed.   Her body still in his other hand he leaned his head down and began to eat her esophagus, enjoying every bite. Because he knows he is uncertain the next time he will be able to feed.   He also knew that no one would ever summon him again, well at least not on purpose anyway.   With that he let the lifeless body fall onto the bed, and slowly slipped back into the shadow from witch he came and then disappeared.

Chapter 1

The day started like a typical Wednesday morning, well at least as typical as they come. The usual 4

o'clock morning coffee before my shit, shower, and shave routine, then off to deal with the fucking

Denver traffic. But something seemed off, I couldn't put my finger on it, but definitely some thing. As

I got out of the shower for some reason I just stared at myself in the mirror, looking at my hair, now

with a salt and pepper blend, and beginning to recede. ' I should dye it naw fuck it, I thought to myself.

" I only have two more years till retirement. " I told myself as I was tying my favorite tie,

trying not to laugh because I know my wife hates it.

" who wears a red plaid tie your a detective not a golfer. "

she would say, and as always just one last check of everything before I go. Suit looks good check,

keys check, gun check, badge check, and wife still sleeping but check. As I check on her I can't help

but admire her, as she lay there. I start to think of the past 30 years, when we first met when we

were both 19 years old, throughout everything, the dating, years of trying to start a family, and let's

not for get the I'm fat stage that still goes on today, even though at 49 she still looks like a teenager,

with her long black hair, and athletic build she got from trying to lose all the " weight " she gained

over the years. I smile and just shake my head and head off to work. It snowed more than it was supposed to overnight, instead of a light dusting like the news said there was at least three inches, not much but it throws off the plows schedule making the roads a bit of a nightmare. Despite the snow packed roads the drive from Denver to Aurora was not bad at all traffic was light with no accidents witch is always a blessing. As I make my way from my car to my office I can't stop thinking to myself why does today feel so different, am I forgetting something.? I grab my third cup of coffee and try to for get about it. While I'm at my desk shuffling through a case file left at my desk, my office door swings open, just I start going over one of the witness statements. It was my partner and one of the newer more younger detectives, Quincy Steadman. Probably my soon to be replacement, he was a good kid though, graduated top of his class from Howard university before enlisting in the air force. He stood around six feet, more muscular than a lot of the other guys, pencil thin mustache, with an extreme shine to his bald head. As he walks in he knocks on the door.

"Good morning boss" he says with an enthusiastic tone.

I take my glasses off, rub my eyes and look up.

"Good morning Steadman" I replied.

he seemed anxious today

"what's up" I ask

"captain wants to see us"

"really this must be important, he never calls us in."

Steadman lets out a fake laugh while I was getting up. As we leave my office, walking past the cubicles and rows of isolated desk everyone was busy either doing paperwork, or on the phone following leads, a good sign I guess. But why the hell is the captain pulling Steadman and I off of a case?

Chapter 2

Steadman and I walked into the captain's office, its a corner office much larger than all the others. Inside there were decorative items that filled the wall both beside and behind him, everything from drawings from his children, to several of awards, and even a couple of deer antlers. The captain around my age however looked much older, stress of the job probably. The captain, captain Drew Fox also a middle aged man and his silvery hair that was well receded. As he leans back in his chair, he places his glasses on top of his head and buried his face in the palms of his hands, rubbing his eyes and then resting the side of his face in his right hand, while adjusting his black tie to be center on his sky blue shirt, and just stares at us for a moment while letting out a deep sigh. Gathering his thoughts he very calmly spoke with his voice a little raspy.

" Murphy, Steadman, I know your wondering why your here."

"Yeah a little" I replied,

"we have a case I want you two on."

Steadman was furious

"You got to be shitting me we already have three cases we're working."

"I know Steadman, I'm pulling you off all of them, we have a possible serial killer and the media is up my ass sideways, this will be priority number one until this asshole is captured or killed."

"Holy shit a serial killer here in Aurora?" I asked.

The captain stands up and straitens his black dress pants to go over the top of his well polished shoes, he walks over and looks out the window of his office, and let's out another sigh.

"I need you two on this, its one of the worst I've ever seen." Fox said with a little concern in his tone, the captain makes his way back to his desk and sits down, opening the middle desk drawer and takes a manilla envelope then slides it across the desk. Steadman and I exchange a quick glance at each other before I reached out to grab it. As we opened the envelope and pull the papers out, on top were the crime scene photos.

"Holy shit he decapitates them?" Steadman asked.

Fox lowers his eyes looking at the floor.

"If only, no he removes the entire esophagus and takes the neck with him."

"So doctor gone crazy?" I ask puzzled by the photos.

"That's just it no surgical marks or cuts of any kind, aside from where the neck used to be."

"And it gets better" Fox continues.

"only one witness so far, he told his caregiver what he saw, are you ready for this?" The captain asked.

"the suspense is killing me"

I say while going to the next photo.

"The witness claims he saw what looks a lot like Voldemort but scarier."

Steadman raised an eyebrow "uhhhh.........come again."

I look at the captain and stand up, its my turn to go look out the window for a second while all this processes. Shaking my head I let out a laugh.

"so we have some nut job dressing up as a Harry Potter character?" I said now starting to pace in front of the window.

"It definitely seems that way, but I haven't done any digging."

"Well lets go dig." I say to Steadman who was still studying the case, he looks up at me shakes his head and rolls his eyes.

"You do know our witness is at Denver mental health right?" He asks.

"Yeah I know but its the only lead we have right now, unless you have a better idea?" I say while opening the door for him, as we walk back across the room heading toward the elevators.

I think to myself walking next to Steadman not saying anything, I didn't have to we both knew this

was big and we both knew it was only a matter of time before this person killed again. I knew

something seemed off and now I know, as we go down the elevators and out to the back of the police

station, we walked across the parking lot to my car a black a Crown Victoria with a spot light on both

driver and passenger side along with the darkly tinted Windows. You know your typical unmarked

police car, as we got in the car I look at Steadman.

"go ahead." I say.

He just grins, we always have a bit of a problem with the radio stations, him with his 90's hip hop

while I prefer Rush Limbaugh. As we arrive at Denver mental health, walking into the lobby it was

fairly empty, it had a black tile floor with a shine you could see your reflection in. Aside from that

two large black leather couches in the center of the room facing a TV mounted on the wall. There

were patients sporadically placed throughout the facility, and a long oak desk at the other end of the

lobby with a receptionist there for processing family, visitors, and of course lets not forget nosey

police officers like ourselves. Upon approaching the desk, the receptionist a young lady who

appeared to be in her early to mid twenty's maybe 5'3", 100lbs, with red shoulder length hair, and she

had one of those smiles that would just light up any room.

"Can I help you gentlemen?" She asked almost to cheerfully.

"We're looking for someone who may have witnessed a homicide." I said while signing into the visitor

log.

"A Mr. Christopher Gomez." Said Steadman.

It took her a second to think about it, then she smiles

"oh the Harry Potter guy, yeah let me go get him."

After only a few minutes she comes back through the double door that separated the lobby from the

rest of the facility. With her an old Hispanic man in a wheelchair, as she wheeled him towards us we

noticed this was probably a lost cause. The man was at least 80 years old and looked to be in a

catatonic state.

"Mr. Gomez?" I asked.

He was unresponsive, just staring into space.

"Yeah he usually dose that unless you talk to him about something he wants to talk about, so good luck he barely talks to anyone."

The young lady told us as she situated his chair in front of a window so he could see outside.

Steadman and I look at each other, Steadman opened the case file and took out his original statement,

. he made.

Chapter 3

I was hesitant at first handing the witness statement over to Murphy, he already looked frustrated

and we hadn't even started the interview. I could tell just by his look, we've worked together now for about five years. As he stands in front of me and beside Mr. Gomez with his hand reached out for

the statement. His hands old and callous, his slightly hunched over posture, his salt and pepper hair

with about a third of it missing from the front. I look him over one more time at his long sleeve white

dress shirt, and brown plaid suit jacket with an ugly plaid tie.

"We want to talk about the murder Mr. Gomez." Murphy says.

finally taking the statement from me, but nothing the man just sat staring out the window "Mr.

Gomez." Murphy says again with a little more frustration in his voice.

"What about lord Voldemort?" I ask walking toward the window.

Mr. Gomez began to scream in terror and starts to have what looked like was a panic attack.

"don't let him get me, don't let him get me!"

"Mr. Gomez nobody is going to get you we just want to know what he looks like." I told him after the

minute or two of panic.

Finally after composing himself he slowly turns his head to look at me, then he takes a deep breath.

"I'm 82 years old, I've fought two wars, and nothing has scared me like this."

"Go on." Murphy says.

"Your not looking for a man, your looking for a demon, I'm telling you this thing is not human."

"Let's go this is ridiculous, a demon are you fucking serious?" I told Murphy.

"So you only saw him with the costume on?" Murphy asked as he opened his notebook.

"No no no you stupid fucking cops you don't get it!" He yells "calm down Mr. Gomez, let's just take it

from the top just tell us where you were and what you saw." Murphy told him.

Mr. Gomez looks at me then to Murphy while slowly adjusting himself in his wheelchair, and

straightening his hospital gown.

"Fine I'll tell you." He says. I take a hold of the back of Mr. Gomez's wheelchair and start to push him

over to the center of the room, placing him next to the longer of the two black leather couches.

Murphy and I sat down as he began to tell us.

"It was last Thursday, I was at the Aurora mall, it was around 7 o'clock."

"OK doing what exactly?" I asked him.

"Shopping my great grand son had a birthday coming up, so I was going to get him some new shoes."

"Please go on Mr. Gomez." Murphy says.

Mr. Gomez then swallows hard and continues to say.

" I was leaving foot locker, and was on my way to the food court to wait for Misty my caregiver she was suppose to pick me up at eight o'clock. That's when I decided to step outside for a cigarette, bad habit I know but I'm 82 years old, so what the hell right."

That comment got a slight chuckle out of both Murphy and I, but then he spoke and had both of us lost for words.

"I was about halfway through my smoke when I saw it."

"Saw what?" Asked Murphy, as he wrote in his notepad.

"If you would shut up and quit interrupting me I'll tell you."

I tried not to laugh but I couldn't help it, Murphy looked at me and grinned.

"I'm standing by a loading dock away from the entrance, you know so I don't piss people off that don't smoke. And out of the corner of my eye I saw something caddy corner to me move in the darkness, so of course it got my interest I looked in that direction, and what I saw next made me literally piss myself." We all laughed at that, then Gomez takes out a cigarette and says.

"Hell let's go outside."

Murphy and I figured it was the least we could do, so I wheeled him across the lobby and out the front door, and across the parking lot into a white gazebo, it had paint missing in some places maybe because of the weather or just from being there for years, I really didn't care either way, as we sat down in the gazebo Mr. Gomez lights his cigarette and started again. "So anyway I'm looking in the darkness and a shadowy mist appears and started to swirl, slowly at first but gradually got faster, slowly rising while it turned."

"It did this until it was at least ten feet, then the black mist stopped and went back down revealing what I thought was a man at first."

Mr. Gomez takes another long drag from his cigarette, his eyes lower as he gets even deeper in his thoughts before continuing on.

"He was about eight foot tall, and wore a hooded black cloak that looked like it was made of the mist he came from, then he pulled the hood down and I will never for get that face it was a face of pure evil. His skin was white, pale white like the moon, he had a bald head, with pieces of skin that had either rotted off or was still decaying. Then their was his eyes they where solid black with three red elliptical pupils in each eye, the very tip of his nose black and decaying, his teeth looked razor sharp and dark yellow, and finally his hands, they were only slightly decaying and his fingers stopped at about mid knuckle then the large black claws took over for the rest of the finger."

"Holy shit, and then what it just stood around?" Murphy asked still taking notes.

"No he moved closer to the loading dock just as the door next to it was beginning to open, a man walked out, looked like he was taking out trash when he was grabbed. This thing grabs him by the throat and in an instant turns back into black mist, completely covers the man, the mist turning quite rapidly around the man, and just as fast as it started the mist vanished along with that thing. The man taking out the trash just laid there by the door with his head just a few feet away." "Mr. Gomez that's one hell of a story." I tell him as he was putting out his cigarette, I started to push him back inside. and while we we're walking Murphy looks at me with his eyebrows raised and closed his notebook. The drive back to the station was long and awkward, as Murphy drove I just sat there looking out the window trying to think of something to say but after that story I had nothing. Murphy didn't either we just drove trying to let this sink in, that the only lead we have is apparently some kind of creature.

"Well what do you think Steadman?" Murphy asked as we were halfway back.

"I think captain fox is going to be pissed when he finds out this is all we got."

"Yeah me to, so screw it I'm starving, I'm feeling Chinese what about you?" Murphy suggested.

"Yeah I could eat." I said.

We pulled into the parking lot at the Aurora mall and drove around to park as close to the food court as possible, luckily it wasn't to bad of a walk. As we got closer we both walked to the side by the loading dock to look around, we just looked and tried to imagine how the hell he came up with a story like that. We didn't look to long before going in and ordering our food, however I noticed Murphy couldn't stop looking out the window.

"What's up boss?" I asked him as I took a bite of sesame chicken.

He picks up one of his egg rolls, and before he takes a bite he shakes his head.

"I just can't believe as busy as this place stays and no one saw anything."

After we finished our food we looked around one more time, even asked a few employees, but of course nobody knew anything. So we got back in the car and continued on to the station. Again awkward and quiet until we got there, it was the first time in years I had ever seen my partner this

belittled over a case.

Chapter 4

Pulling into the police station I glanced over at Steadman to see if he noticed the news van in the

parking lot, almost as soon as I did Steadman started to point.

"You see what I see." He asked.

I nodded "that's why we're going to park in the back lot, with all of the marked police cars." I told him.

he knew that the only way into the building from that entrance you need a code or key card to open

the door. As were pulling in past the gate Steadman looks back over his shoulder.

"What?" I asked.

"Nothing I was just thinking, its only one news van maybe their not here about the murders."

I shook my head.

"three homicides in the Aurora area, no leads and a crazy witness why else would they be here?"

Steadman shrugs his shoulders as we got out of the car, just before opening the door I stop and turn

to Steadman.

"Ready for an ass chewing?" I asked him.

He smiles "let's get it over with." He says as we go through the door.

we walk down the long empty hallway that takes us to a single metal door on the right hand side of the hall, usually we come out of this door just after roll call but neither Steadman or myself wanted media attention, especially with no answers to give them. We walked through the door and across the room, passing in front of a white board and between the podium and the thirty or so desk in the room, to another metal door, also key card access only, this lead right next to captain Fox's office. I take a deep breath, scan my card and wait for the buzz then went into the room, inside it was almost empty only one or two people occupying desk, no one in the cubicles that went down the side of both walls. As we stepped into Fox's office, the captain was sitting behind his desk looking down at a file, his glasses resting at the tip of his nose, he lifted his eyes just looking over his glasses and let's out a sigh, and raised his eyebrows. He closed the file and very calmly spoke. "OK tell me you got something." He said while beginning to stand. "Yeah one nut job for a witness, with one wild story." I said placing my notes on his desk. Fox begins to look over the notes and smirks. "Six eyes now that's something new." Steadman answers, "no captain, six pupils its the part of the eye.........." "Shut up Steadman I don't care!" Fox interrupted, walking over to a smaller desk that was behind him filled with pictures of his wife two children, and two golden retrievers, and in the center a small collection of Scotch. Fox took three glasses and filled them about a quarter of the way up and sits back down, placing a glass in front of Steadman and I. "Is this allowed?" Steadman asked looking at the brown liquid that was placed before him. "No it's not." Fox Says as he took a sip from his glass. Fox gently rotating the glass watching the scotch swirl before finishing, then got up to pour another. "OK so what about the other to murders what do they have in common?" I asked while finally deciding it was OK to sip on the scotch. "Nothing their all different, different races, different religions, different parts of town, and they didn't know each other." Fox said now walking over to his window, overlooking Alameda parkway. "Let's not forget all different occupations as well." I added also standing, and walking to stand next to Fox. Fox sets his glass down on the window seal, then places his hands on his hips, his right hand resting gently on the handle of his black p90 Ruger. He looks at me while he loosens his tie, and very calmly almost in a whisper says. "You know, this is one of those cases that either make you a legend when solve it, or you kill yourself trying." I smiled but knew he was only half joking. I turned and looked at Steadman still sitting at the desk. "Well come on finish that shit and let's go, we have work to do." I told him while walking to the door. Steadman looking dumbfounded at this point, but not hesitating to quickly finish his scotch and stand up. "What exactly are we doing?" "We have no leads, no real witnesses, and no evidence physical or forensic." "I know, but there has to be something somewhere, we are detectives so let's detect shit, you take the most recent victim and I'll look at the other two." I handed Steadman the file for the Aurora mall incident, and walked into my office. I've had some tough cases but this was by far the most baffling 'OK what am I missing?' I thought to myself opening both files and spreading them across my desk. One man white early to mid Thirty's, insurance salesman, no known religion no debts, and no criminal history. Then case two middle eastern woman, married, early to mid forties, religion was Muslim, massive amount of debt, and no criminal history. Insurance salesman was killed in his home, while the house wife was killed in her church parking lot of all places. I looked the files over for god knows how long, just trying to find something, anything, I took my glasses off and tossed them on top of the files, then got up to check on Steadman. "Anything?" I asked walking over to his desk in the center of the room. "Yeah one hell of a fucking headache, I got a black male, late teens, fresh out of high school, Christian religion, and no known enemies." "Well its almost 5:30 what do you say we call it a day and start fresh tomorrow, I think our eyes could use the break?" I said to Steadman placing my hand on his shoulder and giving it a pat. "Sounds good to me, the Broncos play tonight maybe that will take my mind off of this." He replied as he stood up to put on his jacket.

Chapter 5

I decided to leave the case in my filing cabinet, rather then bring work home with me, for two reasons, one I know better and two that is the last case I want my wife Emma to see, its bad enough I see it. "Tomorrow is a new day maybe we will get something." I said to myself as I was locking my office for the night. I made my way back across the room, once again passing the cubicles that outlined two sides of the room, and the three rows of desk in the center, as I pass by Steadman's desk I touched it and gave it a knock. 'We'll get the bastard.' I thought, as I proceeded to my car, ready for this day to be over. On my way to my car I looked around the parking lot and noticed the news van still parked. 'Great now their doing steak outs.' I thought while starting my car. The ride home was a lot better and faster then it was on my way in, the roads were plowed, still icy in places but mostly just wet. Snow still lightly covered the trees as well as the grass, and it was now starting to get dark, the sun setting behind the mountains giving the sky a dark orange hue, its what we call a bronco sunset. Making my way from Aurora to the outskirts of Denver, to my house just off of Colorado Blvd., and just outside the city of Glendale. Driving slowly through my neighborhood looking at my neighbors, that were still outside, some playing with their children, others walking pets. I can't help but wonder how long before the media get a hold of what's going on and puts everyone in fear. But for now I just

shake it off and go home. I finally pulled into my driveway, got out and locked the door, before I start

walking up my driveway and up to the front door. As I'm shuffling through my keys I stop, my heart

sinks, my mind began to race. As I look at my front door slightly propped open, I quickly place my

keys back in my pocket, and draw my glock 19 from its holster. Trying to remain calm as I approach

the door, my heart is pounding, gun in low ready position, I side step to the left and prepare to open

the door. Using my left foot I push the door open and step in, changing from low ready, to ready

position. As I walk in my living room I look side to side clear, now to the bedroom immediately to the

left, side to side, in the closet, that to is clear. Now back out to the living room, down the hall to the

master bedroom, I placed my weapon in my right hand, and used my left to reach for the door knob.

As I do the knob starts turning, immediately both hands back on my gun for better control. Still in

ready position as the door opens. "HOLY CHRIST SCOTT, PUT THAT THING DOWN!"

"Emma your home early, you scared the shit out of me!"

"Out of you, you have your gun out in the house what's going on?" She asked, my heart rate was

slowing down, I re holstered my weapon and pulled her close giving her a kiss on her forehead, then

again on her lips. "The door was propped open and your not suppose to be home for another hour." I

told her walking back to close my front door. "Yeah they canceled my class at the university, so I came

home to make dinner." "OK but the door?" "The element blew in the oven, we need a new one, it

filled the house with smoke, so I opened the door to let it air out." Relieved as I walked back from

closing and locking the door. I turned and looked at Emma, she had such a concerned look on her

face, she knows I never take my gun out of its holster while I'm at home. As she stood there with her

arms crossed, her black hair down just passed her shoulders and eyebrows raised, with the whole you

better start talking look. I walk into the kitchen that's to the right of the living room, open the

refrigerator and grab a beer. "Well?" She asked starting to walk towards the kitchen arms still

crossed. "Well what?" "Well what the hell is going on you just came through our house like you were

hunting one of your bad guys." "Oh my god Scott has someone threatened you?" Staring at her now

standing in front of me on the other side of the kitchen table, I sigh deeply. "No, no threats, just a

case getting to me." I told her finally sipping my beer. "Which one?" "Only one, Fox put me on a new

case and took me off the others." "Why would he do that your a good detective?" "We have a serial killer in Aurora, and its getting to me, its like this guy can't be stopped, he leaves absolutely no evidence." "Wow that's scary, maybe we should go out tonight, you know just to keep your mind on other things." Even tho I appreciated her gesture I knew it wouldn't help, but none the less, I finished my beer and got ready anyway. It may have been paranoia but after changing my clothes, I went through every room in the house just to be sure before leaving.

Chapter 6

After the day we had of getting no where I decided to leave a little earlier than usual, we had one hell of a case and I knew Murphy wouldn't mind. I left the police station the same way I always do, going out the back door the way Murphy and I came in a few hours ago. My car a dark green 2015 Ford explorer parked at the very end next to the marked police cruisers, next to the gate that separated our cars from the public. As I pull around the station I let out a little laugh, as I noticed the news van still in the parking lot. I continued to my apartment not far from work, just a couple of miles away.

Pulling into my apartment complex I drive past the office, and mail boxes that are at the front entrance and to my building. Two buildings down as I get out of my car, and begin heading up stairs to my apartment on the third floor. Just as I'm putting my key in the door, my neighbor who lives across the hall yells to me. "Did you kill them all yet?" For some reason he has a conspiracy theory that the police are trying to kill all black people. So I smile and shake my head as I walked into my apartment, as soon as I walk in and lock the door, princess a stray, that I adopted a few years ago, meows and rubs her black and white face on my leg. Picking her up I walk passed my living room, to the end of the hallway to my bedroom to get a can of food for princess. I open my top dresser drawer and take a can out, opening it and setting both the can of food and princess down next my closest. While I let princess eat I decided to take shower before getting something for myself. Standing in front of the mirror in my bathroom, the shower running and the glass starting to fog I keep wondering how hard this case is going to be to crack. Nevertheless I continued on with my shower, finished and got dressed, walking out of my bedroom down the hall, to the my kitchen on the left of living room. "Ain't this some shit." I say to princess as I'm looking in the refrigerator, with only a couple of cans of soda

and a beer inside. 'I'm sure as hell not cooking' I thought to myself.So I went back out to my car, I'll go

the the Hooters just down the road. That way I can watch the broncos play the falcons while I eat,

not to mention all the eye candy that's there. After getting to Hooters and being seated at the bar,

my waitress came over, a cute little blonde in her twenties. I ordered my wings and a pitcher of beer,

and thought maybe I should talk to the blonde. Probably best if I don't I'm already busy with the case,

and besides I think I'll wait for someone that has a great brain to match her looks. The last thing I

want is to date another idiot who thinks Alaska is an island. I laugh to myself and continue watching

the game and eating my food, I know I can't stay long Murphy probably wants me in early tomorrow.

For a moment I thought about texting or calling Murphy, but decided against it, I know he will call me

if he wants me in early and besides I don't want to bother him while he is at home with his wife.

Chapter 7

"Who the hell is calling at one in the morning?" Emma asked as I was picking up my phone off the nightstand. "Murphy." I answered. "Murphy..... Murphy it's Fox we have a situation how fast can you get here?" Now sitting up and starting to get dressed, I put the captain on speaker phone. "What kind of situation what happened?" "Just get to Denver mental health as soon as possible." Fox told me and then hung up. 'Denver health?' I thought while throwing my shoulder holster on as fast as I could then tying my shoes, then grabbing my jacket on my way out the door. I get into my car and speed as fast as possible through my neighborhood and head towards Denver mental health. Racing down Colorado Blvd. Passing under the streetlights, weaving in and out of traffic with my lights on and sirens blaring. My mind is trying to play out what happened, as I keep thinking of the worst possible scenarios. Then it hits me the mother fucker got to my only witness, he was a nut but the only one we had. As I'm speeding well over 100mph I slow down to give Steadman a call, he answers on the first ring. "Steadman it's Murphy." "Hey yeah I'm already here, your not going to believe this shit." "Its Gomez isn't it?" I asked while getting into the emergency lane on interstate 25 making my way as quickly as I could through the traffic, which wasn't much unless your in a hurry then light traffic is to much. "Just get here." He says and hangs up, what usually is a thirty minute drive from my house I managed to make in a little under twelve. As I turn the corner heading toward the facility, all I could see was flashing blue lights. Now turning off my own lights and siren slowing down as I approach the first set of police cruisers that were blocking the road. I pull up and showed them my badge, they just nodded and backed up letting me in. Driving by I could see they had every road leading to the facility blocked off, with police cars or fire trucks. The scene at Denver health was intense, every direction you looked there was blue, or red lights flashing. Spectators stood behind the yellow police tape, some recording with their phones others just looked on. I pulled up next to Steadman's SUV, where he was waiting on me. I got out of my car and shook Steadman's hand. "Good morning." He said. "Will someone please tell me what the fuck is going on?" I snapped back walking toward the police tape. "Murphy I don't know how but yeah, he got Gomez." "How this place is secure, no one in or out without clearance." Finally at the police tape in front of the building I saw Fox, he walked up handing me a cup of coffee and lifted the yellow tape so Steadman and I could get to the scene. "Corner says time of death was around 23:30." Fox explained. I didn't respond I just quietly walked on, into the facility. Inside it was complete chaos, between forensic taking pictures and dusting for prints, and regular patrol doing crowd control, there was at least 20-25 personal. Steadman and I walking rather hastily to the check in counter, to officers were there questioning the young red haired girl who allowed us to talk with Mr. Gomez just a few short hours ago. She was sitting on the floor next to her desk, her red hair slightly tangled from holding her head or running her fingers through it. "She tell you anything?" I asked as we approached the officers that just finished asking their questions. "Not much, she said everything was fine when he went to bed, until she checked on him a little after midnight." Before I could say anything in a response Fox came out from the double door, pointed and waved for Steadman and I to follow him, into Gomez's room.   There wasn't much inside the room, a dresser against the wall in the corner, a television a couple of feet from that, and then in the other corner of the room a twin bed with Mr. Gomez's body. His head lodged between the bed and the wall just below his barred window, his body still in the bed his torso soaked in blood as well as his sheets. Steadman and I standing in the middle of the room, letting forensics take their pictures and dust for prints. Fox was talking to one of the crime scene investigators about what happened. "OK boys you ready?" Fox asked holding the back of his neck. "Give it to me." Steadman said moving closer to Mr. Gomez. "CSI says we have no forced entry, no prints, no hairs, and only Gomez's blood." "What about that?" I ask, nudging Fox's elbow with mine, while pointing to the surveillance camera in the far corner mounted above the door as you walk in. Fox's eyes widened and then he grins. "Finally a break if we got the son of a bitch on camera." The three of us rush back out to the check in desk to find the red headed girl. She was still there, now being checked out by paramedics. "Excuse me mam." I said stopping the paramedics and grabbing her arm. "Where's the surveillance room?" "Its downstairs in the basement, but I don't have the password I can't play them back, I can only watch live stream." Fox got the manager's contact number so we could view the camera, he said it would take about an hour, plenty of time for Steadman and I to make a coffee run.

"Thank God Starbucks was open, I can't do that gas station coffee." Steadman said as we arrived back at the crime scene. "Rookie." Fox mumbled taking his coffee from Steadman, I looked up at Fox and smiled, and nodded in agreement. Almost an hour and a half later the manager showed up, he was a lot younger then I was expecting. Only in his mid to late thirties, short buzz cut brown hair, well over six foot, and looked to be extremely underweight, but I'm no doctor, I just want him to play the damn tape.

Chapter 8

It felt like an eternity, but only took about five or ten minutes to go from the front desk to the basement. It didn't help when the "manager" kept checking his phone and fumbling over the keys. But finally we managed to get there, we had the manager go back to 21:00 and show us how to go frame by frame. "Can you please wait outside, I'm not sure if you want to see this it could be very graphic." I told the manager as I sat in the chair in front of the surveillance monitors. He thought it over, but only for a moment then left and decided to wait just outside the door. "OK let's do this cross your fingers and hope we get something." I said to Steadman and Fox, then started clicking the button to go to the next frame. Nothing just Gomez sleeping until we get to 22:50 then it started. "What the fuck?" Fox said watching me slowly click from one frame to another. Watching as the barred window turned completely black, and through the cracks of the window you could see the fog, dark black low lying fog. It slowly crept from the window, to the floor until the entire floor was covered with this black fog. Then it sat there barely moving, like when you watch steam come up from a lake or a pond. For several minutes it just did that not moving, not until I got to 23:15. Then it began to slowly turn and come together at the same time, it was like watching a tornado form but from the ground up. Turning slowly and gradually picked up speed and height, until just like Mr. Gomez said, it was about nine or ten feet and spinning rapidly. The just as fast as you could blink your eyes the fog was gone and a manlike creature stood there, wearing the black hooded cloak that looked like it was made from the fog he came from. "The poor son of a bitch wasn't crazy." Looking

at the monitor in amazement, hell we all were we could not believe this thing was real. But in the

back of my mine and I'm sure everyone's in the room, was how the hell are we going to stop this thing?

I began clicking again, watching this creature move forward, not walking tho, it seemed like it was

hovering or gliding across the room until it was at the foot of Gomez's bed. "Look at that shit,

Voldemort my ass its more like Voldemort mixed with Freddy Kruger." I said pausing on the shot we

had of his face, Steadman placed his hands on his hips. "Yeah but a whole hell of a lot uglier."

Looking back at the monitor I continued to click. The creature crept closer moving up the side of the

bed, until it was standing next to Gomez's shoulder. Then it leaned down, his face next to Gomez's

ear. "He's whispering something." Fox said. Then it happened, the creature's hand grabbed Gomez's

throat, and in one swift motion tore his throat out, head rolling to the edge of the bed and between

the wall. "Oh my god....." "Hold on Steadman look at this." The creature's mouth opened, and his jaw

started to extend until it was wide enough to cover the top portion of the torso. "Oh fuck this I'm

going to be sick!" Steadman said walking quite quickly out of the room. "It looks like he's feeding,

there is no surgery he somehow sucks everything from the inside out." Fox said, now taking the seat

next to me. "Look at this he doesn't take the throat with him he eats it." I pointed out. "Aahh shit

Murphy let's go find Steadman I think we've seen plenty." I nodded and got up, walking to the door.

"We're going to need a copy of that footage." I told the manager as I exited the room We found

Steadman outside getting some air, and the three of us where trying to understand what we just

watched. I took a few minutes to clear my head before going back inside to check on how our copy of

the footage was going. Steadman and Fox stayed outside discussing the case. It only took the

manager a few minutes to have the footage burns on a CD for us, after he handed it to me I began

once again walking out of the surveillance room. As I did I paused for a moment, thinking about this

case, and wondering what the hell we could do about this thing. I leaned with my back against the

wall, gently tapping the DVD in the palm of my hand. I ran my fingers through my hair and started

walking again, I was halfway down the hall when I hear laughter, a child's laugh. At this point I'm

confused so I turn around, there was a girl, a young girl maybe eight or nine years old. With shoulder

length dirty blonde hair and blue eyes, she was barefoot and wearing a hospital gown. "Hey sweetie

are you lost, where's your mommy?" I asked her. "I'm not lost, but your in trouble." "I'm in trouble how's that?" The little girl smiled. "You know Shay-tan Alzzilal is going to kill you." She said to me and began skipping down the hall and around the corner. ' what the fuck?' I thought, I ran after her but when I turned the corner I ran into Steadman almost knocking him to the ground. "Woe slow down boss what's the hurry?" "Fuck off Steadman where's the little girl, I just saw come this way." "What little girl?" "The little girl that just came by here two seconds ago." "Are you OK , I've been standing here for almost ten minutes waiting on you, and the only person that came around that corner was you." I handed the DVD over to Steadman and rubbed my eyes. "This case must be getting to me, after seeing that I think my imagination is getting the best of me." I told him, placing my glasses back on my face after giving them a quick wipe.

"I don't know about you Steadman, but I'm going to need more coffee before we go to the station."

Chapter 9

I don't know what the hell got to Murphy, maybe it's the case, maybe it's his age. Whatever it is had him come around the corner at Denver health like he was chasing a suspect. But either way I thought it would be best to just shrug it off like nothing happened, after all we have bigger fish to fry. I told Murphy I would get more coffee, if he wanted to just go to the station. He was more than happy to oblige, I think he needed the drive to help get his mind back in the game. It took almost an hour and a half to get the coffee and then to the station. I made a personal note to never again go to Starbucks at 07:00 in the morning. "What took so long?" Murphy asked as soon as I walked into Fox's office. I threw up my free hand and rolled my eyes, while using my other hand to place the cup holder with the three coffees on Fox's desk. "I hit rush hour, both on the highway and at the coffee shop." I said, handing them both their cups. Taking a sip from his coffee Fox started. "OK first off what the hell is that thing, and second how in God's name are we going to take it down?" Neither Murphy or I spoke, we just sat there trying to think of what we could do or say, then finally Murphy spoke up. "I guess we could see what happens if we look online." I scowled at Murphy. "And look up what exactly?" I asked him. "Shay-tan Alzzilal, its what the little girl called it." "Oh Christ Murph there was no girl, I was there the whole time, from the time you went to the back, to the time you almost put me on my ass." "Damn it Quincy I know what I saw, and I know what she said." Fox slammed his hand down on his desk. "OK ladies if your almost finished, we do have a case, one that we don't need to be arguing over one we need to solve, I don't care if it was a delusion or not Murphy follow the damn lead, and Steadman what do you got?" I thought for a moment, then cleared my throat. "Well all the murders do have one thing in common, they all take place at night or pretty close to it." "So what, is this thing some kind of vampire or something?" "Its possible captain, I mean after all up until a few hours ago

we thought our only witness was mentally insane." Murphy stood up and began to stretch, and

finishing his coffee. "A vampire really?" He asked me. "Look Murph I don't know I'm just throwing it

out there, I mean we got a thing I'm assuming it is a he based off the face, that turns into some kind

of fog, then we have you seeing little girls, so hell why not maybe we can research and compare notes,

and maybe build from there." Fox looked at me then to Murphy, then back to me. "I can't believe

this, its like the fucking twilight zone. Oh what the hell we have nothing else to go on." "Soooooo?" I

said also standing up. "So, so what get your asses to work and find something, get on the internet, go

to the library, I don't care just, just something anything."

Murphy and I nodded at each other, and started to leave Fox's office, his phone was ringing anyway.

Fox stopped us as we we're at the door. "Murph, Steadman hold on." Fox said hanging up the phone

and sitting back at his desk. "What's up?" Murphy asked. "We have another murder, same M.O."

"What, its broad daylight." "I know so it may have just blew the whole vampire idea out of the

water." "So where to boss?" I asked Fox. "Aurora theater, had an employee taking out the trash and

never came back." "Aurora theater wow I haven't been there since the shooting."

"That's not all Murphy, when he didn't come back someone went to check on him and caught a

glimpse of our guy."

"So another witness?" I rhetorically asked. Fox nodded and stood back up, walking over to his

Scotch. Murphy and I left and where on our way to the crime scene, as soon as we got in Murphy's

car I asked. "How the hell are we really going to stop this thing." "I don't know Quincy, I don't know,

but I do know if we don't try the bodies are just going to keep piling up, we're already up to five and I

don't think this thing plans on stopping anytime soon." "Shay-tan Alzzll." Murphy muttered while we

were going down the road. "What?" "Shay-tan Alzzll, that's what the little girl called it, I can't get it

out of my head. It has to be what its called, or its name." Murphy said, I stared at him with a puzzled

look on my face. "Look Murphy the girl...." "I'm not crazy I really did see her, and she really did say it."

He said interrupting me. I said nothing in response, until we arrived at the scene it was probably good

for both of us, we were both on edge. Captain Fox was right with everything going on right now, the

last thing we need to be doing is arguing.

Chapter 10

Steadman and I arrive at the scene, its the typical chaos, five or so police cars blue lights flashing. Yellow police tape around the perimeter of the dumpster, half a dozen or so spectators, some crying, some recording with phones or other devices, while others just watch, both in horror and amazement. "Homicide." I said as I was showing the other officers my badge and walking under the police tape, with Steadman not far behind me. As we get closer to the dumpster, I approach one of the uniformed officers, he had to be a newbie. He was young couldn't be a day older than twenty one, in his dark blue uniform, badge and shoes were polished up nicely, as if he were fresh out of the academy. "What we got?" Steadman asked him. "The victim Jacob McMahon, white male, 19 years old, was taking the trash out and when he was gone for over an hour, another employee came out and this is what she found." "Poor girl." I said, as I started to examine the body. "This ones different, where's the head?" "In the dumpster detective Steadman, I was told not to move anything until the scene was documented." "What kind of sicko does this?" The officer asked me, I looked at him and placed my hand on his shoulder. "Trust me kid you don't want to know." Steadman and I really didn't need to ask anymore questions, but following protocol we did, just to make sure we didn't miss anything. Now we have left is to question the witness just as soon as the paramedics are finished giving her a one over. Turning back to the officer I asked. "Has anyone notified the boys parents?"

"No sir not yet." He responded. I walked back across the parking lot, over to my car where Steadman was waiting. "Steadman make sure that after the corner picks up the body, the parents of this boy are notified, make rookie do it." I told him, I knew he was tired of doing it, he's been doing it since he became a detective. "Gladly boss!" He said with a little enthusiasm in his voice, I knew he needed the break. Hell the worst part of your job as a police officer, is notifying the next of kin. Especially when its a child, its something you have to do face to face. And the response is always the same, its always anger, confusion, and they always want answers, answers that you don't have. No matter how many times you do it, it always seems to tug at your heart. So I know Steadman was grateful for not having to do it this time. "Poor bastard, he said this will be his first time notifying next of kin." Steadman said walking back over to me grinning from ear to ear. We both let out a little laugh, not because it was funny, but because we knew what he was getting ready to deal with, your first one is always the hardest. "How do you think we should do this witness?" Asked Steadman, as he leaned against my car. "You can do it if you want, I need to get some food I'm starving." I told him, as I gave him a notebook and got into my car.

Chapter 11

After Murphy abandoned me, I walked over to the ambulance, opened the notebook and took a pen out of my shirt pocket, and introduced myself. "Hello I'm detective Quincy Steadman, with the Aurora police department and if you don't mind I'd like to ask you a few questions." The girl sat there in the back of the ambulance still crying, she had long curly blonde hair, and bright green eyes, and black streaks from her make-up running down her face with her tears, but she still managed to nod her head yes, while wiping tears from her eyes. "Great we'll start with the basics, first off what's your name and how old are you?"

"My name is Summer Andrews, and I'm seventeen years old."

"OK miss Andrews, take your time and just tell me what happened." She composed her self and thought about it. "Your going to think I'm crazy." She said still trying clean the make-up off her face.

"No mam miss Andrews, I just want to know exactly what happened I don't care how crazy it may sound, trust me it makes sense to me." She looked at me and took in a deep breath and her voice still a little shakey. "Jacob told me he was going to take out the trash, that's like our code for us to go make out behind the dumpster, he grabs some trash and waits for me. Then we come back in before anyone notice's, but this time he was taking forever to come back inside. So I thought he was waiting for me to come back, I told my boss I was going to help Jacob with the trash and. And." She began to weep uncontrollably, and her hand were starting to shake as well. Also Murphy pulled back into the parking lot and was walking toward us.

"Please miss Andrews go on." I said. Murphy now standing next to me, with a ' damn what the hell did I miss ' Look on his face. Murphy reached into the bag he was carrying and pulls out a bottle of

water and offers it to her. She took a sip of water and started calming back down. "Thank you." She

said to Murphy, then she looked back at me and started to continue on. "So when I came back out, I

could hear wind, like really strong wind you know how it makes that howling sound. But it was only

coming from the dumpster, I told Jacob I didn't think he was funny. So I opened the gate, and right

next to the dumpster was Jacob. He was standing in fog, but like it was black not white. And it was

moving really fast all around him." She paused taking another sip of water. "Then a face showed up

right next to him, nothing else just a face right next to his." Murphy cut her off. "So just a face and no

body?" He asked. "That's right, and then it opened its mouth like really wide, then the fog got thick,

so thick I couldn't see Jacob anymore. It stayed that way for I don't know like thirty seconds, then it

just disappeared. And there was Jacob lying next to the dumpster, without a head and his fingers

were twitching, oh god." She started to cry again, Murphy looked at me and took the notebook.

"Thank you miss Andrews, why don't you go home and try and get some rest." He told her. I got up

and handed her a card, for a crisis counseling hotline I'm sure she's going to need. I stood up and very

quietly walked with Murphy back to the car. "Well what do you think?" I asked Murphy, while

getting into the passenger seat.

Murphy ignored my question, instead he was busy scowling down at my notes going over the

interview. Ten minutes we sat there, till finally Murphy cleared his throat, while closing the notebook

he turns his head towards me ever so slightly looking over his glasses. "Quincy. What the fuck are we

missing?" I didn't respond instead we sat quite, motionless, neither of us had an answer. Still not

saying a word Murphy started the car and drove off, heading back to the station. It was by far the

longest and quietest ride ever. We needed a break, a tip, something. Bodies were piling up fast and

we still had no answers. Back at the station we were back in Fox's office, he now had a map of the city

on the wall behind his desk just to the right of his scotch table. He had a red thumb tack placed were

all the victims were found. After briefing him Murphy and I walked over and took a look. "Fuck this is

like trying to put a puzzle together in the dark." I mumbled, leaning closer to the map trying to find

something that could give is some kind of help. With no luck I decided to go to my desk and see if I

had any messages, I needed the break as I sit down I looked back at Fox's office. Fox was going to

lunch, and Murphy staid still looking at the map, I rolled my eyes 'he's wasting his time. ' I thought as

I turned on my computer. While going through pointless email after pointless email I here Murphy shouting from Fox's office. "HOLY FUCKING SAINT MARY!" I got up from my desk and was walking to see what the hell he was yelling about, as I was walking Fox was getting off the elevator with his lunch. "FUCKING SAINT MARY!" He shouted again. Fox and I stepped into the office. "Murphy what the hell are you screaming about?" "Captain I got a lead look at the map" "OK I'm looking, what am I looking at?" I stood there silently with a bewildered look waiting for Murphy to enlighten us. "Five victims, five different locations and what do they all have in common?" "Nothing Murph we went over this already." "No not nothing, look at all five murders, they all are five to ten miles away from saint Mary's Catholic church. And look at this the murder locations form almost a perfect circle around the church." "Coincidence?" I asked now standing next to him also looking at the map. Murphy my partner, my friend, my role model, I have worked with him a little over five years and I can read him like a book. I could tell just by looking at him, he didn't think the church was a coincidence, so before he said anything I spoke up. "Well Scott let's go to church." Murphy didn't say anything, he didn't have to he just smiled, grabbed his jacket and left the room. Fox looked at me, I could tell he was pissed. "Quincy what the hell are you doing?" "Just following a lead." "Your going on a wild goose chase is what your doing." "That may be captain, but you know Murphy, if he thinks he has something he's going to look into it weather you like it or not. Besides this whole damn case has been a wild goose chase." Fox rolling his eyes and throwing his hands up, walked over to his desk and sat down. "I hope you two find something." "So do I Drew, so do I." I didn't say anything else, I just left the office quietly and went to my desk. I shut down my computer, and put on my jacket and walked outside. Murphy already had the car running and was waiting. "So how did he take it." "He is pissed of course, he thinks we are wasting time." Murphy nodded his head in agreement and drove off. I waved to Murphy as he exited the parking lot. While I was walking to my car and pulling my keys from my pants pocket. I couldn't help but wonder how much more interesting this was going to get before, it was all over.

Chapter 12

I sent Steadman a text when I got to my car, telling him we'll check out the church tomorrow, and that I was calling it a day. It took all of five minutes before I saw Steadman in my rear view walking to my car. He gave me the scoop on how pissed Fox was, but at the same time I really didn't care. I knew that saint Mary's has to have some kind of information about this. There is no way this is coincidence, but I wasn't going to let Fox get to me I just shrugged off what Steadman told me, about it being a complete waste of time and drove off. Halfway home and my mind starts racing, thought after thought, I didn't want to go home I wanted to go to the church now. But it was probably closed and I needed to get some rest, I really haven't ate or slept worth a damn since I got assigned to this case. But couldn't stop thinking about it, I could still see the map in the back of my head, saint Mary's Catholic church and five red thumb tacks in almost a perfect circle around it. "No way its coincidence." I said to myself as I got out of my car and began walking up my driveway. Walking through my front door I could see Emma standing in the kitchen in front of the stove, as I walk through the foyer and into the living room. "Your late." Emma says turning around. I smiled a fake smile and walked into the kitchen with her, opening my refrigerator and taking out a beer. "Really as soon as you walk through the door, your not going to eat first?" "Not much of an appetite I'll eat later." I told her now twisting the cap off the beer and walking back into the living room. I pick up the remote control and sit down in my easy chair and turned on the news. Just as the news was coming on I was caught off guard, the top story that they were covering was a serial killer in Aurora and how Aurora police are not giving any details. Taking a sip of my beer and then setting it on the coffee table in front of me, along with my glasses. "Oh Christ I can't believe this, this is great." I said louder than I should have. Taking another sip of beer, this time finishing over half of it and getting up to get another. On my way into the kitchen I finished the other half, and grabbed another. "Bad day?"

Emma asked still cooking. My eyes rolled. "You have know idea." I told her and went back to my

chair. Emma was smart maybe a little to smart, she finished what she was doing then walked into the

living room. Sitting on the couch and looking at the TV. "This has been on all day, they want to know

why the Aurora police is keeping information from the public." She informed me, not taking her eyes

off the TV. "You going to tell me about it?" "Emma you know I don't like telling you about my cases,

and besides you wouldn't believe me even if I did tell you." "Scott we have been together for thirty

years." "Fine Emma, we have something called Shay-tan alzzll going around tearing peoples heads off,

now I'm not sure what the hell a Shay-tan alzzll is but I'm going to find out." Emma looked at me not

saying a word, she nods her head and smiles. "Your not crazy I've heard of it before." She says now

getting up and going back into the kitchen. "Whoa whoa whoa, wait, what, your telling me you know

what this thing is?" "Yeah I heard about him in one of my classes at university, I don't remember

much about him. Only that he originally came from the middle East, Israel I believe."

I was dumbfounded at what she was saying, I couldn't believe she knew what this thing was. "So are

you telling me you know how to stop it?" I asked while getting yet another beer. "Hell I don't know

Scott, I'll have to go through my old text books and see. I'm not doing it tonight and neither are you,

now come on enough with the beer you need to eat something." As much as I didn't want to, I had to

admit she was right. I needed to eat something and more importantly needed to get some sleep.

Sitting down now at the dinner table I looked up at my wife, my conscience telling me not to but I had

to ask. "So Em, that book, do you know where it is?" Emma scowled at me. "Damn it Scott, your at

home not at work. I promise I will look for it tomorrow." The rest of dinner was quiet, little to no

conversation. However I did get a much needed shower and I went as far as turning off my phone, so

I could get some rest.

Chapter 13

The following morning I got to the station around 8:30. As I got out of my car Steadman was getting out of his SUV just a few spaces over. "Good morning Quincy." "Good morning boss, I brought coffee and doughnuts." he said to me still not fully awake. "Oh yay cop food." I said back laughing slightly. Then Steadman asked. "When do you want to go?" "9 or 9:30 because I want to be sure someone will be there." We didn't bother going inside, it wasn't that cold outside so we just stood in the parking lot enjoying our coffee and doughnuts. We waited until 9:15 before Steadman and I started to make our way to the church. According to the map and the GPS it wasn't that far of a drive only fifteen minutes, however an hour and a half later we were still looking for it. Finally we stopped for more coffee, and asked the clerks if they knew were the church was. "Your looking for saint Mary's? Its not there anymore, they moved it back in the 50's." I heard from behind me. When I turned around, there was a girl looked like she was still a teenager, she was short maybe a little over five feet, with blonde hair pulled up tightly in a bun, her eyes where green, bright green almost a neon color. "Yeah that's right, do you know where we can find it?" The girl pointed East. "Your way off, they moved it to Limon." She told us. "But the map and the GPS?" Steadman said back. "All I know is they moved it to Limon, why your GPS brought you here I don't know." "Do you know why they moved it?" I asked her, now stepping out of the way for the other customers. She shrugs her shoulders. "I don't know, I know my Grandpa used to go on and on about it being haunted, if you believe in that kind of stuff." "So where in Limon is it?" "Not sure exactly, I know you can see it from the road, just go East on I 70 you'll know it when you see it." I let out a deep sigh. "So that's it just East until we see it." The girl now looking a bit annoyed. "Yeah pretty much." She told us, then she sidestepped and left the gas station. Steadman and I finished our purchase, and walked out. We took maybe two or three steps outside the building, then heard a click. The click you would hear from a door being locked or unlocked, both Steadman and I turned around towards the building. "What the fuck?" Steadman said looking at me. I couldn't believe it either, the building we were just in was empty. No lights on, the doors were locked, and it looked as if it had been abandoned for years. I set my coffee down and walked up to the door. Pressing my face against the glass, so I could look in. It was empty, completely empty, there were no shelves, the coolers were empty, and dust and spider webs were everywhere. I took a step back, turned and looked at Steadman. "OK two questions Steadman, one did that just really happen? And two how the hell did we get coffee?" Steadman thought for a moment, then raised an eyebrow he took the lid off his cup and smiled saying. "Whatever happened we still got coffee so watch out!" We both laughed hysterically but then quickly realized the reality of what happened, gaining our composer and proceeded to the car. After getting in and rerouting ourselves toward the right direction to the church, it occurred to Steadman and I that we were in some serious shit. As we listen to the GPS making our way out to limon witch is far out of our jurisdiction, but nevertheless we had a lead and we had to follow it. It wasn't until we were about ten miles from the state line when we saw it, a small church just off of I - 70 just like the girl said. "Well I'll be damned." Steadman said pointing south at an old church, that looked run down. It was a small church, it looked like it my have been someone's house at some point, a typical ranch style house in the middle of nowhere. The only thing that made it stand out was a small cross mounted on the roof, aside from that nothing it was just a house. In the middle of a field and a single dirt road going from the interstate to the church, hell not even a parking lot. As we take the exit and start heading South on the road leading towards the church, it wasn't hard to find it was the only road on the exit. It led to either a gas station, two farm houses, or the church. After passing row after row of corn fields, for two or three miles. We found a narrow dirt road that went into one of the corn fields. Another mile surrounded by corn, when we finally emerged from the corn five minutes later. There it was in the middle of the field, looking back in my rear view mirror at the corn. Then in front back at the wide open field with the house that had been converted into a church. The road led straight to the front door, I pulled my car off the road just south of the front doors and parked. Steadman and I got out to take a look before trying to gain entry. It was a lot bigger up close, a large two story house, it seemed to be made entirely of wood. Old wood it was warped and rotten, it leaned unevenly on its

foundation as if ready to collapse at any moment the windows that weren't missing where boarded

up. Walking up to the steps I loosened my tie, looking at Steadman I placed my foot down on the first

step, it let out a soft drawn out squeak. At the front Steadman and I stood there just about to knock,

when we heard a very faint voice it sounded like an old man. "No need for knocking, for all are

welcome here." The voice said from inside. Steadman turned the door knob opening the door, it too

let out a squeak. Inside was a very large and very empty, only three pews at the front. And in front of

them a single podium, the windows that were boarded up from the outside, were old stained glass

with pictures of various biblical scenes. "OK I'm confused, this was a house right?" Steadman

whispered. I speechless as well, on the inside it was a massive cathedral, still rundown but huge. Still

not saying a word and beginning to walk down the aisle towards the front I see a light on in what

looked like an office of some kind just to the left. We got closer maybe two or three yards from the

podium, when the light in the office turns off and the door slowly swung open. Out stepped an old

man, a very old man. He stood about six feet tall, wearing a black clergy robe. His long white hair

exceeding down past his shoulders, stopping at the small of his back. With a silver mustache and

beard that went just past the center of his chest. His skin was pale and full of wrinkles, he walked

ever so slowly moving closer to Steadman and I. In a very thick accent I couldn't place he began to

speak, his speech slow and shakey. "I haven't had company in years, tell me what brings you here

today?" He said beginning to sit in the middle pew in the front. "My name is detective Murphy and

this is my partner detective Steadman, and we're hear to follow up on a possible led."

The man lowered his eyes, and with a slightly confused look, looked back at me. "I see, well what can

I do for you gentlemen?" "We are here investigating multiple murders, the only suspect we have, we

believe is called Shay-tan alzzll."

The old man lifted his head, his eyes wide and yet didn't seem surprised. "Shay-tan alzzll, I haven't

heard that name in years."

"What can you tell us about him?" Steadman asked, now pulling a pen from his shirt pocket. "You

want to know how to stop him don't you, to be honest I don't think you can. I've heard rumors, but

I'm just an old man." He smiled his teeth yellow and quite crooked. "Please father any information would be greatly appreciated." "Very well but listen and listen carefully, I'm very old and I don't want to have to repeat myself."

Chapter 14

The old man now crossing his legs, and leaning back in the pew let out a deep sigh and cleared his throat. "Almudammirat kabira." He said softly. "Come again?" I asked, looking at Murphy to see if he was as lost as I was. "Almudammirat kabira, it means the great destroyer in Arabic. Its also what he used to be called at least around 1300bc. It was the Passover, when the Israelites were being freed from Egypt. He was sent to kill all first born in Egypt who's house was not marked with blood." "Yes father we know the story."

"No you know the story as it was written and corrupted by man, as man saw fit. Do you really think everything was accurately documented in the bible, if so my boy you are a bigger fool than I thought." The old man then stood up not saying a word and began walking back to his office, Murphy and I followed. "Can I offer you detectives some tea?" We both nodded and took a seat in his office. He began making tea, as he started to continue. "When he came down that day in Egypt his mission was simple, kill where there is no blood and he did. Then because of the free will given to him by God, he decided it wasn't enough. You see he was programmed to kill evil, and what he thinks is evil and what actually is, is very different."

The old man now placing a cup of tea in front of Murphy and I, he then sat down letting out a grown on his way into his chair. "What he thinks is evil?" I asked raising an eyebrow and taking a sip of the tea. "That's right, I take it you are familiar with the ten commandments?" I nodded, not saying a word. "You see my boy the ten commandments always existed, they just weren't actually written in stone until Moses went to the top of the mountain. But nevertheless as the story goes, that if you follow the commandments then you in turn are following God's will. Well that's not how the destroyer saw it, not at all." "You see he thinks that any and all corruption is punishable by death. This is why he went from the great destroyer to the shadow demon. He went from killing by command and to feed only, to now he kills to feed, and to cure what he thinks is corrupt." Murphy now scratching his head and trying to make sense of everything, placed his notebook down on the desk and asked what we both were thinking. "So what does he think is corrupt?" The old man frowned, clearing his throat once again. "Almost everything, you see once he has fed and gotten his strength back he will go on a killing spree unlike any you've ever seen." I sat up in my chair. "Wait what do you mean after he has fed?" "You see detective he is weak right now, very weak he must feed every six days or he starts to decay, if he misses more than two feedings before he is fully strengthened the decaying will rapidly take over him, forcing him to go into a hibernation type state." "Hibernation, for how long?" I asked. "Until he is summoned." "People summon this thing?" "Yes every few hundred years someone will, thinking they can use him for their own purposes. However when he is summoned he has to feed and well they're right there so that's his first meal." Murphy stood up and stretched, then decided to chime in. "OK, OK, hold on why dose he only feed on the throat, I mean what's up with that?" The old man started laughing slightly coughing while doing so. "It's the soul detective, he feeds on the soul, have you ever heard the saying that your eyes are the window to the soul?" "Of course I have." Murphy replied. "That's just the window, your soul lives deep inside of you. He removes the throat and the head and sucks the soul out, sometimes eating the throat and esophagus just to make sure he has consumed the entire soul." "So why every six days and how many more times before he is regenerated." I asked him now standing up to stretch my legs as well. "Six days three to digest the soul and three for his strength to build. He feeds until he is no longer decaying, it varies depending on how long its been since he was last summoned, but usually ten feedings before he is fully restored." I sat back in my chair rubbing my eyes, and looking at the priest. "OK father so every six days, its five days since the last victim. So does he just pick someone at random, how does he choose?" "He is probably looking for his next victim now, he looks for the most corrupt souls he can find." At this point Murphy threw both his hands in the air. "Well why the hell doesn't he go to a prison, plenty of corruption there?" "Yes there is detective, but he won't risk being exposed to the light. Prisons have large amounts of light, he won't go near large amounts of light until he is fully restored." "So what's with light?" I asked closing my notebook now as well. "Its like an allergy, it weakens him to where he can't travel. You see he can only travel from one dark place to another, even when fully restored he must travel quickly thorough illuminated places. But not all light works it must be bright, the moonlight, street lights, things such as that will have no effect on him. But a spotlight from a prison, or the bright florescent light all throughout the prison with no darkness to hide in, that's why he stays away." "So is no one safe?" I asked. "Few are safe detective, because he was created by God he cannot come to hallowed ground, and he cannot slay the truly innocent."

"What the hell would be considered truly innocent to this monster?" Murphy snapped back.

"Children detective, children are truly innocent." "So we are all just fucked." I said, covering my mouth at the same time. The priest smiled. "No your not fucked detective, there is a way to capture him. He must be in his humanlike form then you must shine large amounts of light on him so he cannot change, and be sure there is no darkness around. But a word of caution if you do he will both bless you and curse you." "I'm sorry what do you mean bless and curse?" Murphy asked. "When he is captured he will grant you one wish, anything you want except for bringing back the dead. He will grant your wish but make you immortal." "Immortal that doesn't sound so bad, has anyone ever caught him before?" I asked nudging Murphy's elbow. "I was just a boy that night in Egypt, playing with my brother he told me I couldn't catch him. We began running around our house hiding from one another, I thought I heard him on the other side of a chair. So I jumped towards his direction yelling 'I got you.' But I went over the chair and out the window, when I looked up there he was in full human form, I was laying on my stomach, arms extended, holding on to his ankles." The priest finished his tea and kept on. "The destroyer looked at me and knelt down, face to face with him I knew what he was and I was terrified. He leaned in close to my ear and said ' yes you got me, what do you wish for most. ' I didn't have to think I was tired of being a slave. My wish was to leave Egypt, me and my people. After I told him he stood up, still looking at me. Then he smiled, changed from human form to his ghostlike mist and vanished into the night. The next day we left Egypt, all of us that was thousands of years ago." Murphy and I sat quite, both in shock and amazement at the story. But I still couldn't help but ask. "What about the second?" "Ah yes that was a couple hundred years after me, a little girl, I don't know much about her story. Except that she has powers of her own. But her wish however, was to have the destroyer as her guardian. She is the only one that I know of that can summon him and not be killed, she can also give him orders from time to time when he is not feeding." Murphy jumped up. "A little girl, is she around nine with blonde hair?" "Not now with that Murph." I said rolling my eyes. "Its hard to say detective I only saw her once and that was years ago." Murphy cut his eyes at me, and the back to the priest. "So what powers, what can she do?" Murphy asked. The priest was now making a second cup of tea, tapping his spoon on the side of the and sitting back down. "She's psychic, she can make people see things that are not there. As well as do things they don't want to do, she can also read minds." I looked at Murphy. "The gas station." I said. "You've already encountered her?" The priest asked, now drawing his focus on Murphy. "Yes once at Denver mental health, and again at a gas station not to far from here." Murphy explained both stories, the priest slowly nodding his head while listing before finally saying. "Well then detectives I would be careful, she probably knows your trying to stop her guardian. As I said she is psychic, and very powerful, don't be surprised if your eyes start playing tricks on you." Murphy and I thanked the priest, and walked back to the car. Standing at the passenger side door, I looked at Murphy. "Well what do you think?"

"I think that priest lied to you Steadman, I think we are totally fucked." I didn't say anything in response, just looked around one more time and got in the car.

Chapter 15

Nancy Hopkins finished getting dressed, making sure she wasn't forgetting anything. She straitened her little black dress, reapplied her make-up and ran her fingers through her long blonde hair trying to fix it as best she could. She was after all supposed to be having a girls night out, at least that's what she told her husband. Before leaving the hotel room she kisses her lover one more time. "See you at work." She says to him while walking out the door. Nancy made it home just before 2am, her husband was sleeping on the couch with a beer still in his hand and the TV still on. She tiptoes past him, down the hall and into the bedroom. Once again removing her clothes before getting into bed, her husband would be getting up for work soon and she wanted to make it look like she had been home for hours. Her eyes were getting heavy, and she was just about asleep when she heard a very faint whisper. "Adulterer." It said. Nancy's eyes popped open, she got up and looked around the room but saw nothing, down the hall her husband still slept. Now she couldn't sleep wide awake she decided to watch TV in her room. An hour later she was in grossed with her television program. Once again her eyes were getting heavy, as she starts to nod off she hears it again, only slightly louder. "Adulterer and a liar." She opened her eyes as her husband was turning on the lights, she looked at him trying to pretend that she had been sleeping and it was he that woke her. In the back of her mind however a slight panic, wondering if she was going insane, or if her husband knew. Nancy pondered this for a moment or two, thinking there's no way, she and her lover were both married and they were both so careful. Either way she didn't get much sleep, as she dozed off for the third time it was 4am and her alarm clock was going off. Exhausted from a late night out and lack of sleep, Nancy took a quick shower pressed her uniform and headed off to work. After arriving to work at the Glendale police department, she did her usual check in at role call, making sure her patrol car was ready with the proper equipment, and testing her lights and sirens. Finally getting into her car she radioed in to dispatch so she could start her day. The day was unusually slow, a minor traffic stop here and there, and only a couple of well fair checks. The rest of the day was to be spent catching up

on paperwork, Nancy was a third of the way through her second affidavit when her phone buzzed.

"Hey beautiful." Said the text. It was her lover, a lieutenant for the department. Still thinking about

the odd incident that happened at her place last night she replied. "Hey did you tell anyone about

us?" "What no why?" Nancy decided not to tell him the details. "Lol just asking, I'll text you later."

Nancy turned her phone off and placed it in her purse and finished her paperwork, now that her day

ended all she wanted to do was go home and get some sleep. When Nancy got home she changed

from her police uniform into some sweatpants and one of her husband's T-shirts, she poured a glass

of wine and sat down on the couch and turned on the 6 o'clock news. Thinking to herself what a

shame it was that Aurora, not to far away was having so many murders. Turning her phone back on

and still partly watching the news, her buzzed again she had two new text messages one from her

husband, and one from her lover. "Picking up some overtime baby won't be home till around 11."

Nancy smiled and checked the message from her lover. "Are we meeting up tonight?" Nancy smiled

again and put her phone down, all she wanted to do was relax. She sat on the couch going from

channel to channel, until finally stopping on one of her favorite reality shows that was just starting.

Nancy got up to pour another glass of wine, while she was putting the wine bottle back in her

refrigerator someone knocked at her door. 'Who the hell could this be.' She wondered. Walking to

the door, she opened it but no one was there. Nancy shrugged and went back in to the kitchen

grabbing the bottle of wine. ' screw it. ' she thought, taking the bottle with her back into the living

room. After channel surfing for a couple of hours Nancy poured another glass of wine, and since the

sun had set she walked around her house sipping her wine and closing the blinds and curtains.

Feeling pretty buzzed she headed back to the living room, slightly stumbling back to the couch and

sitting back in front of the TV. As she sat there working on her wine and not really paying any

attention to what was on the TV, out of the corner of her eye she saw the curtain next to the TV lift

slightly and fall back down almost as if a gentle breeze had blown it. At first Nancy didn't think

anything of it, but when she went to take her next sip she paused just as the glass touched her lips. '

wait a minute I closed all the windows. ' She thought putting her glass back down. Nancy then got up

and walked over, she lifted the curtain and looked behind it but there was nothing, she checked the

window as well but it was closed and locked just as she thought. Nancy shook her head. "OK that's enough wine for you Nancy." She said out loud to her self, turning back to the couch. As she turned Nancy saw a silhouette of a man standing in front of her, with his head down looking at the floor. He very slowly lifted his head, in the darkness of the room Nancy couldn't make out a face, she could only see six glowing red slits. Nancy now frozen with fear decided to try and speak to the man. "What are you doing here, you know I'm a police officer." She said. The man said nothing but took a step closer toward Nancy extending his arm slowly reaching for her. "Did you hear me I'm a police officer, think about what your doing." She said again hoping to deter the man who had some how gotten into her house However in an instant, faster then Nancy could blink her eyes. His monstrous hand was around her throat, he pulled Nancy close to him. They were face to face only millimeters kept their nose's from touching, slowly tightening his grip until he knew she could barely breathe. Nancy struggling to breathe, gasping for air grabbed the creature by the forearm trying to pull herself free. Pulling and scratching his arm did not phase him, with his other hand he pulled Nancy's hair gently over her ear and began to whisper. "How long did you think your sins would go unpunished." "How long did you think." "Judgement is upon you now for your sins are many." The creature said. Nancy's eyes widened as she looked into the creatures eyes, the red glowing slits slowly widened as he stretched out his arm and raised her off the ground and began to tighten his grip. Nancy struggling to breathe was gasping for air, squirming and violently clawing at his arm she realized it was useless. Her eyes began rolling back and her body was relaxing as she started to lose consciousness. Now pulling her back close to him, he took his other arm and placed the palm of his hand under Nancy's chin and pushed up while the other arm pulled down and toward him. He could feel her bones breaking and the muscles tearing, then the flesh also began to tear. Blood dripped out of her throat and on to his hand, running down his arm to his elbow before dripping on the floor. Still pushing, and pushing then finally the head came free, still attached to the body the creature let it hang dangling between Nancy's shoulder blades, held on by the skin that didn't tear. He opened his mouth wide enough to cover the area where the head was, and began to feed on the life giving soul that was within. After finishing he paused, "only four more, then I can cleanse the world." He thought to himself, as he threw the now lifeless body down on the floor in front of the couch knocking over the bottle of wine. Now that he has fed he starts to transform, his body turning to a black fog so he could easily slip through the cracks of the window. The sun will be up soon and he is not yet strong enough to try and take on daylight, so he slips through the window to find a dark enough place to rest until its

time to feed again.

Chapter 16

I got back into the car and fastened my seat belt, looking at Steadman I knew he was thinking the same thing. That we probably are not getting out of this alive, the sun now beginning to set I reached for my coffee so I could dump it out. Picking up the cup it felt lighter then I remember when we went in, I removed the lid and looked in, it was empty. "Fucking psychics." I said looking at Steadman, showing him the empty cup. Putting both hands in the air he let out a little chuckle and shook his head, and put his seat belt on as well.

Driving back to the station so I could drop Steadman off at his car before heading home, it was getting late and I knew Emma was going to be pissed. As we drove back through the corn, and was making our way back to the interstate my cell phone lit up in the center console, I started reaching for my phone when Steadman gave my hand a quick slap. "What are you doing, your driving?" He asked. "Come on." "No I won't come on, we arrest people for that. Here I'll get it." I threw my hand up. "Whatever." I told him. Steadman picked up my phone and checked my message. "Oh fuck boss your wife is freaking out, she said Glendale police are everywhere." "What, what happened?" "All she said is come home now, something happened to your neighbor Nancy." "Nancy?" I asked glancing over at him. "Let's go, you can drop me off later." Steadman said to me as I turned on my lights and sirens, and sped up to well over the speed limit. Weaving in and out of traffic, my mind was racing. As I merged from interstate 70 getting on to Colfax and then to airport Blvd. Glancing over at Steadman. "This is to close to home, Nancy lived right next to me." I told Steadman, not saying a word he nodded his head as we continued heading towards my home. I don't really know how to explain it or if it even makes any since, but tonight seemed darker then usual I don't know maybe it was just my nerves. After all ever since we were assigned the case it has been murder after murder, crime scene after crime scene with little to no time in between. As I was making the turn from Colorado Blvd. On to Mexico when we saw the blue lights from the Glendale police cruisers, as well as the several spectators most of whom I have known over the years, and the crime scene tape that went right up to the side of my house. The police presence was so active and so large I couldn't even

park in my driveway, I had to park some two or three houses down and walk up to where my house

was. While approaching my house I was stopped by one of the Glendale officers. "Sir that's close

enough." He told me. "I live next door, Nancy and her husband are good friends of mine." The

officer looked at me and rolled his eyes. "You can go to your house but that's it I don't need you or

anyone else interfering with my investigation." I threw my hand up. "OK, OK, OK, but can I just ask,

was she decapitated?" The officer raised an eyebrow and lifted the police tape. "Get in here."

Steadman and I walked under the police line, then the officer grabbed me by my shoulders and pulled

me close to him bringing his mouth next to my ear. "You better tell me how the fuck you know that,

we haven't made any statement to the press and this is something only we and the killer would

know." "Just calm down I work for Aurora police department, I think our cases might be related."

Then he loosened his grip and gave me a slight shake. "I hope so because I've never seen anything

like this before." "Give me ten minutes let me check on my wife and get her calmed down then we

can compare notes." Not saying a word the officer gave me a nod and lifted the tape once more,

Steadman and I proceeded toward my house. Emma had the front door open and the glass screen

door closed, I could see her frantically pacing back and forth going from the living room to the kitchen

and then back to the living room. As Steadman and I got closer Emma saw us through the screen door,

as she did she ran out giving both Steadman and I a hug. "Oh my god how bad is it, they wouldn't let

me anywhere near the house, they wouldn't tell me anything either how bad is it?" Steadman and I

looked at each other then back to Emma, Steadman took a deep breath and cleared his throat. "Its

um going to be fine." Emma looked furious. "Don't bull shit me Quincy, you either Scott tell me the

truth, I've been around law enforcement long enough to know when its something, now tell me how

bad is it?" Now it was my turn, clearing my throat I looked at Emma then to the floor. "Emma darling,

Nancy was a good person......" "No, no, god no, not Nancy do you know who did it?" "Shay-tan

Alzzl." Steadman whispered. Emma began crying hysterically, her body became overwhelmed as she

fell backwards onto the couch, burying her face in her hand she wept for almost fifteen minutes

around the same time the doorbell rang. Emma got up and walked into our bedroom to try and

compose herself, Steadman went to answer the door. Three Glendale police officers came in, all

looked relatively young early to mid Thirty's if that. "Please come in have a seat." I told them. Two of them sat down the other just leaned against the wall by the front door, as I began to explain

everything I knew about Shay-tan Alzzl. As I'm telling the story about the murders Steadman and I

had with our case, I told them everything else, about the little girl, the priest, the church, everything.

I was maybe halfway into explaining everything when Emma came back into the room, no longer

crying. She didn't say a word she calmly walked passed everyone and into the kitchen, then returned

placing five beers on the table in the living room along with a book. Very calmly she whispered.

"There has to be a way to kill this thing find out and kill it." She said and then walked back into the

bedroom. This grabbed everyone's attention, with one hand I picked up the book and with the other a

beer and gave it to Steadman. Now taking a sip of my own beer I looked at the book and read the

title aloud. "Ancient Egypt's gods, beliefs, and superstitions." By this time all three officers were

sitting closely as if I were going to read them a bed time story, the thought made me chuckle a bit.

But as I began looking through the book I stumble across chapter eight, a chapter titled Shay-tan

Alzzll. I quickly skimmed through the chapter, until a certain sentence caught my eye. "Check this

out." I said and started to read aloud. "Although Shay-tan Alzzll is said to be immortal, it is also

believed he can be killed. He is not immune to death, its believed that he will live forever but if

someone or something were to inflict a life threatening injury it will indeed kill him."

After reading one of the officers chimed in. "So what your saying is this thing lives until someone can

grow a pair and off him?" Closing the book I took my glasses off and tossed them on the table. "It

would appear so." I told him now handing him and his colleagues a beer, he looked bewildered as if it

were poison. "We can't take that we are on duty." He said to me, Steadman and I laughed. "With

what the five of us are up against." Steadman said back sarcastically. The officer closest to me

slammed his hand down on his knee. "Fuck it give me a beer, its not everyday you find out that

monsters are real and you have to fight them, what next vampires and zombies?" He said waving his

hands and picking up the beer that was in front of him. The other two officers started laughing and

grabbed theirs as well. I think at that point we all knew we were not police officers anymore, at least

not while this thing was alive. The officers called in to and said to dispatch that something came up

and to take them off duty, then we all made the phone call to our supervisors saying that for the next

few days we couldn't come in. Even if it meant disciplinary actions, at that time we knew it didn't

matter we knew what had to be done. I got everyone another beer and sat back down, as we twisted our caps we clanked our bottles together. "Till the end." One of the officers shouted. "Till the end."

We all said back in agreement. The ruckus was enough to make Emma come out of the bedroom.

"What the hell is going on?" She asked. I got up and walked over to her placing my one free hand on

her shoulder. "We are going to hunt this thing down, we're going to kill the son of a bitch." I told her,

and as I did there was another glass clank and one officer even yelled. "Hoorah." "Hoorah." We all

repeated. Emma started to tear up but some how managed to hold back the tears, instead she smiled

while taking my hand off her shoulder giving it quick kiss before letting it go. Once more not saying a

word walked back to the bedroom, and as she got to the doorway she turned. "Promise all of you will

come back." She whispered. Nobody said a word, we just nodded our heads as Emma walked back

into the bedroom and closed the door.

Chapter 17

We stayed up the rest of the night getting to know one another, Steadman and I of course already knew each other. As for the other three, officer Danielle Hernandez a cute little Hispanic girl that couldn't have been no older then twenty one. Probably fresh out of the academy, with her was her partner Jake Milliani. A former Marine however he looked like he has been a police officer for a few years, he was older than Danielle but not by much. Then finally the officer who stopped me at my front door. Officer Julio Bloodhound a cocky little son of a bitch, that didn't pull any punches he was your typical super cop wannabe. It wasn't until around 3am when we decided to start sobering up, we figured if we were going to fatally wound this thing we should probably get better weapons. I knew that if we explained everything to Fox he would give us access to some serious firepower, or at least that was the plan. As the clock made its way from three to seven the other officers thought it would be best to head home and try and explain this to their loved ones. As for Steadman and I we got back into my car and began heading to the station, so we could inform Fox. Exhausted from the lack of sleep we had to stop for coffee on the way, while standing in line waiting to pay. "So even if Fox does approve us for the weapons, how the hell are we going to find this thing." Steadman asked.

Hearing the concern in his voice, with no answer to give him I remained quite not saying a word instead just nodded my head as if I were agreeing with him. But to be honest I wasn't even sure if Fox would approve us for the weapons, and if he didn't then what, we couldn't hunt this thing with a few service pistols, not after seeing what this thing could do. Not to mention Steadman was right, how the hell were we going to find this thing. It attacks at different times of night, hell one was during the day. Also almost every attack was in a different part of the city, the most recent one was outside of Aurora. This had my mind going a million miles an hour all the way to the station.

Chapter 18

Arriving at the station now still a little buzzed, but sober for the most part. At least for me I wasn't sure about Steadman but he looked as if he were good enough. Now the only thing we had to do was finish composing ourselves and go talk to Fox, we kept our heads down trying not to draw to much attention too ourselves as we made our way through the station, mostly from the media personal and not so much our fellow officers. But I still didn't want much attention from them either the less questions the better, I'm sure Steadman felt the same way. We preceded through the station, up the elevator to the third floor. Then down the hall were our offices were, as we entered the doorway we could see Fox's office door was open. We walked in still trying not to draw attention, I told Steadman that we needed to get everything about the case out of our desks then meet back up so we could talk to Fox. Steadman nodded and we began walking as if it were a normal day. "STEADMAN, MURPHY, MY OFFICE NOW!" Fox yelled slamming his office door. The room grew quiet, so quiet you could hear a pin drop. Nevertheless Steadman and I gathered our things from our desks, now standing in front of Fox's office waiting for Steadman. Fox however wasn't waiting he walked up and slammed his hand against the glass office door and waved for me to come in. I opened the door and stuck my head in. "Hey boss Steadman is jus......" Fox quickly interrupted. "I don't care get your ass in here and sit down." I hadn't seen Fox this pissed off in years, I knew better then to say anything instead I calmly walked over and took a seat in front of his desk. Fox was pacing back and forth going from his desk back to the window, that is until Steadman came in. "Get your ass in here." Fox yelled as soon as he saw Steadman, Steadman also not saying a word taking his seat next to me, then Fox started. "OK first off where the hell have you to been, you missed roll call, you didn't check in with me or with dispatch. We have another murder in Glendale with the same M.O. I've got the press up my ass, and now internal affairs trying to say that you two are dirty cops, so someone please tell me what the hell is going on." Steadman cleared his throat, and started to explain. "Look boss we....." Fox interrupted once more. "And not to menti..... Wait are you two drunk?" I rolled my eyes. "Fox we might have had a little bit to drink last night but we are fine, but we did get some valuable information and we really need your help." I could see Fox starting to calm down, he quit pacing the floor. He walked over to his desk still standing he placed both hands on his desk. "Well let's hear it then." He said now sitting down, kicking both feet up on his desk and leaning back interlocking his fingers and placing them behind his head. "Well...we found out you can kill this thing." Fox leaned forward. "Kill it how?" Now Steadman stood up, helping himself to some of Fox's scotch. "Well apparently the damn thin lives for ever but can be killed, so basically it just keeps living until someone or something kills it. Imagine never being able to die by old age, or illnesses, only by an intended act." Fox leaned forward now rubbing his face with his hands. "OK so how the hell are we going to kill it, I mean you saw what it can do, you know how fast it can move." "Yeah we haven't got that far yet, but we did however recruit three Glendale officers that want to help take this thing down. That's where we need your help." "My help with what, what do you need?" He said as he focused his look on me. "Weapons, if we could get weapons preferably a couple automatic m-16's, or maybe some flash bangs." "Are you crazy with the media, and internal affairs breathing down my neck, if I approved you two for that without solid evidence or a warrant. I will have the Chief himself in my ass, I can cover for you and say your undercover so you don't have to worry about dispatch or roll call. But to sign off on that kind of firepower I'm sorry I will lose my job." Now frustrated I quickly stood up. "Damn it captain." "Look Murphy I can't approve anything like that.. But if you were working a case or cases and needed access to the evidence room who knows what you could find in there." Fox said smiling as his eyes widened. I sat back down while doing so I gave Fox's hand a quick slap. "You know come to think of it I do have quite a few cases I'm working on, and the evidence is overwhelming I might need to take some things out for court or for DNA testing." Fox smiling from ear to ear now. "Well then detective Murphy why didn't you say so, now that, that is something I can sign off on." Immediately I walked out of Fox's office and went to my office to get some evidence bags in case I needed them, walking back into the office I gave Fox a wink. "Come on Steadman let's go we're done here." Steadman nodded, placing the half empty glass on Fox's desk and followed me out the door. Just as I stepped out of Fox's office I paused for a moment, turned around and went back in. "What now Murph?" Fox asked still sitting at his desk. I looked around the room. "That." I said walking over and removing the map from the wall, not saying another word I rolled it up as if were some kind of old treasure map and left again. "Now

then." I said to Steadman. "Let's head to the basement."

Chapter 19

Murphy and Steadman stepped off the elevator and into the basement, it was a narrow hall with only two doors at the other end. The door on the left was were all the paperwork was kept, everything from the departments financial records, copies of officers reports, case files and arrest records. On the right was the evidence room, anything from weapons to drugs or whatever else that was confiscated from criminals. With only one officer in charge of both rooms Steadman and Murphy had a plan, Steadman walked up to the officer. "Hey captain wants to see you, he told me to take care of this till you get back." The officer not convinced looked at Murphy and then to Steadman. "Come on man let's hurry this shit up, do you want to radio him or what I got things to check out." Murphy snapped, throwing his hands up and then reaching for the radio on the desk. The officer pulled the radio just out of Murphy's reach. "Calm down I'm going." He replied, opening and holding the door so Murphy and Steadman could get into the evidence room, then casually walked down the hall to the elevator. Murphy and Steadman waited until they knew the elevator was on the way up. Steadman looked at Murphy and laughed. "I can't believe that actually worked." "Yeah me either, but that means we probably don't have much time Quincy." "What all are you trying to get Murph?" "Anything you think can kill this thing." Murphy and Steadman then began looking through the evidence room, Murphy on one side and Steadman on the other. As they were looking it felt like a complete waste of time, it was mostly drugs a few knives here and there and a couple of hand guns witch they already had. As they searched on it took about an hour, then Steadman called out to Murphy. "Jackpot, come check this out." "What is it Quincy?" Murphy asked making his way to the other side of the room. "Must be from some drug dealer or something." When Murphy finally maid it over to the other side where Steadman was, he was in shock. He saw at least ten weapons, a couple AR-15's, AK-47's, and a couple sawed off shotgun's. "Well damn." He said picking up one of the shotguns. "But hold on Murph it gets better." Steadman said, pulling the top off of a plywood box. "Shit are those frag grenades?" "Yep six of them." Murphy smiled and started to load the weapons into a duffle bag that he brought with him from his office, as he was loading the second rifle into the bag Steadman picked up one of the AR-15's. Steadman stared at the rifle with a blank stare on his face, a look as if he were in a daze not in his right mind. His face showing no emotion, just a blank stare. Then his eyes rolled to the back of his head, Steadman picked up a loaded magazine and loaded it into the rifle. The rifle now loaded and with his eyes still rolled into the back of his head, he reached up and pulled the charging handle then released it loading a round in the chamber. "Quincy what the hell are you doing, that's not funny." Slowly Steadman raised the rifle pointing it at Murphy, with his eyes still rolled he smiles and begun to speak slightly hissing while he spoke. "Ssshaytan Alzzllss doesn't like being hunted we sshall kill all who try." "Quincy what the hell." Murphy sidestepped and grabbed the barrel of the rifle, pushing it up towards the ceiling. Murphy now fighting with not only his partner but friend, Steadman and Murphy are face to face struggling over the weapon. "Quincy what the hell come back to me, don't do this." As Murphy said that the lights flickered off then on, back off and then on and when they came on the second time there was the little girl. Murphy's heart dropped, the girl was standing behind Steadman. Her eyes too where rolled back, her right arm extended with her fingers spread apart. As she moved her arm up Steadman's arm also went up, she was controlling him. Murphy and Steadman continued to fight over the rifle, at least five minutes went by witch felt like an eternity before Murphy saw his opportunity. The lights still flickering on and off as the girl shifted Steadman's body to Murphy's right side, Murphy pushes up and to the right as hard as he could, forcing Steadman into the shelving next to him. With Steadman now on the floor and the rifle in Murphy's hands, Murphy used the stock of the AR 15 slamming it into the side of the little girls head striking her in her left temple. Just as the rifle made contact with the girl's head every light in the room went out, it was pitch black and Murphy couldn't see anything. Murphy also couldn't tell where or what Steadman was doing, Murphy readied the rifle just in case he was forced to shoot his partner or the girl. Looking for a place to step in the darkness, dragging his feet across the floor as he walked so he wouldn't trip over anything. In only a few steps Murphy managed to find a light switch, to his relief when he turned it on Steadman appeared to be unconscious. ' Thank God I don't have to shoot him. ' he thought to himself. When Murphy turned around to set the rifle down behind him the lights flickered off then on, when the lights came back on the girl was standing in front of Murphy just inches away from his face. The girl still in the same hospital gown as before, only this time it seemed dirty and torn in places. With blood slowly running down the side of her face she reached her hands out to Murphy as if expecting a hug, cocking her head slightly to the left. Her blue eyes began to shine, much like a cats eyes reflecting off the light. She leaned closer, Murphy took a step back aiming the rifle center mass on her chest. She cocked her head back straight and screamed. "Hadha im yantah baed." The light then started flickering extremely fast on then off, on off, on off, then on again and with that the girl was gone.Murphy let out a sigh of relief, and set the rifle down. His hands shaking almost uncontrollably he placed his hands on top of his head and fell to the floor, and began to weep kicking the rifle across the room. The rifle slid across the floor, stopping within arms reach of Steadman. Steadman let out a groan. "Grrrr, what the hell happened?" He asked. "What the hell do you mean what happened, you almost killed me." "Wait what no I didn't, I was showing you grenades then I passed out I must be dehydrated." "Dehydrated, your telling me you don't remember anything?" "No Scott, we were looking at the grenades then everything went black then I woke up what the hell happened?" Murphy started to cry again, Steadman was flummoxed as he walked over placing his hand on Murphy's back. "Hey come on I'll help you get the guns so we can get the hell out of here." Murphy didn't say a word, instead he nodded his head in agreement and got up from the floor. Steadman helped Murphy to his feet and back across the room, they finished loading the weapons into the bag in complete silence. On their way out of the evidence room Murphy paused for a moment, to once again take in everything that just happened. "You good?" Asked Steadman. "Yeah I'm fine, just a bit overwhelmed that's all." After they got back to the car and loaded the weapons into the trunk, now sitting in the drives seat Murphy paused once more. Looking over to Steadman, he felt he composed enough and began to tell Steadman what all took place in the evidence room.

Chapter 20

I was absolutely astonished at what Murphy told me, while we were driving back to his house. I just couldn't believe it, did I really just try and kill my friend, my partner, my mentor. I sat there for the remainder of the ride trying to wrap my head around the story, almost to his house and Murphy finally breaks the silence.

"Look Quincy, it could have happened to me too apparently the priest was right she is very powerful."

"I know Scott, but I tried to kill you."

"No you didn't Quincy, you weren't in control she was. She was the one trying to kill me."

"Yeah but its still fucked up."

"Yes Quincy, yes it is. But what are we going to do about it , now that's the question."

"Hell Murph I'm still trying to decide who is more of a threat, the little girl or Shay-tan Alzzll."

"Ha I know that's right." Murphy said.

as we pulled into his driveway, while I was getting out of Murphy's car I noticed two more crown Vic's in his driveway as well as a charcoal gray SUV, an explorer I think, parked on the side of the road just a couple of feet from his mailbox.

"I see Glendale's finest are already here." I said pointing to the crown Vic's.

Murphy paying more attention to getting to his front door than the vehicles, he just walked by them and me not saying anything. We stood outside his door for a moment or two, we could hear a lot of talking and laughing from inside. Murphy looked down at the doorknob, letting out a heavy sigh as he opened the door and stepped in. Walking into Murphy's house everyone was laughing, joking, and seemed to be having a good time, I was eager to join in with the socializing, one because I needed to try and relax and two Danielle was hot and single. Murphy quickly shot that idea right out of my head, standing in the middle of his living room, one hand on his hip, the other resting on the handle of his gun.

"Well I'm glad we can have a good time, while a homicidal monster is literally killing people at random."

"Murphy look..."

"No fuck you Jacob I was almost killed a couple of hours ago, so can we at least be professional."
With that Murphy slammed his hand against the wall and went into his bedroom, Emma quickly
followed behind him.

"Almost killed, what is he talking about?" Danielle asked, while getting up from the couch.

"Its a long story." I replied.

After several minutes of explaining what happened earlier, Murphy emerged from his bedroom.
Once again looking around the room, not speaking to any of us but nodding his head. I thought I
would try and lighten the mood, so I got the keys from Murphy and went back out to the car. I
opened the trunk and pulled out the duffle bag that Murphy and I loaded to the gills with weapons, as
well as the box of grenades and took them into the house. When I went back inside Murphy had the
map spread out on his coffee table, and the other officers were studying it. As I got closer Murphy
turned making eye contact with me, then he looked at the bag, then at the box.

"Hey check this out." Murphy said, still looking at me and pointed at the table.

I walked forward setting the box on the table, and the bag on the floor next to it.

"Oooh what's this you brought goodies?" Danielle asked.

At the same time Jake didn't hesitate to open the box containing the grenades. Julio unzipped the
duffle bag, and everybody's jaw dropped at the sight of the weapons.

"Holy shit, Scott tell me these aren't stolen!" Julio asked.

Murphy smiled, taking an ar15 out of the bag.

"Of course not." He said, holding the rifle up as if he were trying to get a better look at it.

Murphy set the rifle back in the bag, and held his fingers in the air making a quotation gesture.

"This is evidence I'm taking to court, or something like that."

Julio rolled his eyes, Jake cracked a smile and moved the box to the floor. We must have spent hours
trying to devise a plane on how we would find the monster, that was the hard part we already knew
how we were going to kill it. Jake suggested an L shaped ambush, it was brilliant we all thought so.

But still the big problem how do we find it.

Chapter 21

We must have went over a million different plans on how to try and lure this thing out, but everyone

of them was a dead end the truth was there was no way of knowing when or where it was going to

attack. After hours of deliberation it seemed as if we were going nowhere, and that we just wasted

all that time coming up with ideas, ideas with absolutely no merit. While Danielle, Jake, and Julio

studied the map and the book trying to come up with fresh ideas, Steadman was pacing the living

room while I stood off to the side in my hallway just in front of my bedroom. I had nothing, no ideas,

at least nothing we hadn't already gone over, so I was standing and watching everyone. With my

hands on my hips, occasionally tapping the handle of my gun with my pinky. I was ready to give up,

all of us where risking so much, risking our lives, our careers, our time with friends and family and for

what? To try and find a monster that we knew so little about, something that has been around for

thousands of years. As my doubt started to consume me I noticed it wasn't just me. Julio was poking

the map repeatedly with his index finger, Jake seemed to be doing a full examination of the weapons,

while Quincy and Danielle were beginning to flirt back and forth in the kitchen. I started to walk

towards the living room to take one last look at the map before I said the hell with it, as I was sitting

down next to Julio, Emma finally came out of our bedroom she had been in there since I had my mild

breakdown. Just as my butt hit the seat Emma spoke very soft almost a whisper.

"I got it, I know how to beat him."

This got everyone's attention back on track, I stood back up and walked over to Emma.

"What do you mean you've got it, we have been over this for hours." "I know sweetie." She said to

me as she gave me a quick peck on the cheek.

She walked over and sat down next to Julio, as the rest of us congregated around her.

"OK let's hear it." I said to her.

"I was just thinking, you know about everything that's been going on. Everything everyone has been

talking about, everything that I've heard, but it was you Scott you and Steadman had the answer all along."

Steadman and I exchanged a glance.

"Emma what the hell are you talking about?" I asked her.

"Well the night Nancy was killed you said you were coming back from talking to a priest right?"

I nodded my head, I didn't know where she was going with this but she certainty had my interest as well as everyone else's in the room.

"Well you also said that the priest said that every couple hundred years or so someone is stupid enough to summon it. What if we were that stupid, you could summon him and kill him when he shows up." She said.

My mouth fell open, I couldn't believe what she just told me we had the answer this whole time. I couldn't say anything to anyone I simply sat back, watching Emma run her fingers through her black hair showing a little bit of grey at her roots. ' time to dye it again' I thought as she pulled it into a ponytail. As she did Danielle cleared her throat and spoke up.

"OK that's great and all but how do we summon him?" She asked.

Emma without hesitation tightened her hair tie one more time, the reached into her front pocket and pulled out a piece of paper. She set on the table and walked over to me, another peck on the cheek followed by a smile.

"That's it, that's all I have I'm going to get started on dinner I take it everyone is staying?" Emma asked walking to the kitchen.

"Oh no mam not me, I have to go home I've got two dogs to feed and walk. But I will come back first thing in the morning." Jake said, putting on his jacket. "OK sounds good we will see you tomorrow then." Emma said.

Jake shook everyone's hand and walked out the door and got into his white crown Victoria and drove off. As he did Steadman picked the paper up off the table and unfolded it.

"Um boss we got a problem we don't speak Arabic, and this whole thing is in Arabic." He said handing the paper to me.

"Emma what the hell Arabic?"

"Ha oh yeah sorry Scott but that's all it said online, just to recite that out loud and he will show up. I don't know what it means but I sure as hell wasn't going to say it."

' great ' I thought to myself, I folded the paper back up and placed it in my pocket.

After dinner Steadman, Julio and I went out to my garage to try and find the inflatable mattresses Emma and I use when we go camping. It didn't take us long to find them maybe all of five minutes, we had them placed on the floor in the middle of the garage. While Steadman and Julio were blowing up the mattresses and checking them for holes, I walked over to the other side of the garage where I kept a cooler.

"What ya got there boss?" Steadman asked, when I opened it.

"Stress relief." I told him, pulling out a bottle of Jack Daniels

"Nice." Julio said, as he and Steadman walked over.

We probably spent a good hour shooting the shit before getting the mattresses and going back inside.

Back inside Emma and Danielle found their way to a bottle of wine, they were laughing and exchanging stories about god knows what. It was at that moment that I thought to myself, that maybe we might just have this thing beat.

Chapter 22

Jake walked outside and gave Murphy one last wave, as he approached his crown Vic he made a quick glance left then right and then left again. After making it to his car he did a quick peak in the window, circled the car and checked underneath to make sure there were no explosives present. Most people gave him bazaar looks whenever he did this, but then again most people didn't know what happened in Iraq. Although he had been out of the Marines for a little over three years it was still a habit, one that has saved his ass on more than one occasion. Now that his inspection was completed he got into the car and started it, after backing out of Murphy's driveway he stopped on the side of the road and reached down to his 4 o'clock position on his waist and removed his colt 1911 from his holster and placed it in a holster he mounted on the side of his center console. Then it was time to continue his commute to Littleton, again out of habit he would check his mirrors frequently looking to make sure nobody was following him and looking around at every red light to see if anyone would try and approach his car. Finally after making the 30 minute trip in 45 minutes because of rush hour he was home, he had a small two bedroom one bath ranch style house just off of Broadway and only about ten minutes from the interstate. As Jake pulled in his driveway he smiled, he could already hear his two dobermans half pint and tiny barking. When Jake got closer to the door he could hear them scratching at the door and whining, Jake unlocked his door and opened it when he was immediately ambushed by half pint and tiny jumping as high as they could onto him licking him and running their bodies against him. Jake raised both his arms and used one to try and pet both dogs while at the same time using his other to close the door.

"Who's my good girls?" Jake said.

Half pint and tiny began to bark and howl as Jake walked through his living room to his kitchen, where he left the two leashes on the counter.Jake quickly grabbed both leashes and struggled to put them on the collars of his dogs who wouldn't stay still, filled with excitement and needing to relieve themselves he finally managed to get both leashes on and walk out the door. As they walked his marine instinct still kicked in, looking on the roof tops of all the other houses, looking especially closer

if someone happened to be wearing a vest. Jake tried to fight the urge to be so alert he would try and

do things to keep him from thinking about it. He would constantly pet his dogs, check his phone, or

even play with his fidget spinner. Anything to keep his mind off of the war, maybe an hour of this

went by and the dogs were finally done with there business and it was time to go back inside. After

removing the leashes from the dogs both half pint and tiny jumped on his couch and laid down, Jake

walked over to his refrigerator opening it and looking inside. Jake rolled his eyes

"Let's see." He said to himself.

"Milk, Chinese, pizza, I don't know what that even is." He continued.

Going from the refrigerator to the cabinet above the stove he found a bottle of vodka.

"JACKPOT!" He yelled. Taking the bottle out and walking to the couch where half pint and tiny where

laying, he sat down and took a long swig. Smacking his lips and wiping his mouth and yet he still had

another dilemma, where the hell was the remote.

"Scoot your fat ass over." He told tiny pushing her aside.

Just as Jake pushed her he found the remote between the cushions, he reached for it and as he did he

felt a small piece of paper.

Jake turned on CNN and then looked at the paper, it was a photo, a photo of him in Iraq he turned it

over.

On the back it had writing.

"November 10, 2004 Fallujah, Iraq 4th battalion, operation al - fair." Jake sat there motionless staring

at the photo of him and his unit, his eyes began to water as he took another long swig of the vodka.

As tears began to run down his cheeks he stood up and set both the bottle and the picture on the

counter next to his refrigerator, and walked out the front door to his car. Again looking left then right

then left, he started his inspection all over again. When it was completed this time he simply just

unlocked the door grabbing his 1911, and stuffed it back into his holster and went back inside. After

going back in side he picked back up the photo and his vodka, and sat back down on the couch next to

his dogs. Jake stared at CNN on the TV, watching them cover multiple stories not really paying

attention but just staring. Jake looked down at the photo once again, and once again took a long sip

of his vodka. As he did Jake reached down to his 1911 removing it from the holster. Another long swig and this time looking into the bottle as he were looking for something he had lost, his eyebrows

lowered and he took yet another sip. Now clutching the photo as tight as he could, he took another

sip and looked at the picture once again. Tears now poured from his face, down his cheek and began

dripping on to the photo. Jake with the 1911 still in his lap picked it up, looking at front to back and

pointed the barrel at his face and then away from him. With one more sip he reached up and pulled

the slide back, watching a round eject from the chamber and loading a fresh one. Now Jake knew it

was loaded, no question as he took another sip and pointed it between his eyes. Staring down the

barrel of his weapon he thought of Iraq, everyone he served with, everyone he lost he took anther sip

then placed the gun to his right ear, then to his forehead, then under his chin, then finally putting it in

his mouth. With his gun still in his mouth Jake slowly starts to squeeze the trigger, with the trigger

almost fully pulled Jake closes his eyes and tightens his grip on the handle. While he closes his eyes as

tight as he can, he takes a deep breath trying to prepare himself for what's coming. His tears now a

steady stream running down his face, his hands were shaking causing the barrel of the gun to bang

against his teeth. Jake bit down on the barrel, and felt a cold wet feeling on his neck. Letting go of

the trigger, Jake took the gun out of his mouth and opened his eyes. When Jake looked to his side, he

saw tiny looking at him while half pint lay on the floor looking up at him as well. Tiny began to whine

while nudging his hand with her nose.

"It's OK girl not today, not today." He said to tiny as he rubbed her head just behind the ear.

Jake got up off the couch and walked back into the kitchen, he dropped the magazine out of his gun

and ejected the round that was in the chamber. Leaving the gun on the counter he put the bottle of

vodka back in the cabinet.

Jake now on the phone ordering yet another pizza and somewhat paying attention to CNN, a

breaking news update caught his eye. They were covering the latest tragedy in Syria, a couple US

Marines were killed in an explosion.

"Yeah that's fine just send it over." He told the person on the phone.

Jake hung the phone up and walked over, again sitting on the couch. As he watched them cover the

story he kept thinking how bad he wanted to be there, to be a Marine again, to kick ass one more

time. Engrossed with CNN Jake was distracted when his cell phone buzzed in his pocket, it was a text

message from Murphy.

"Think we just got a break tell you everything in the morning, we will have coffee ready."

Jake smiled then looked at half pint and tiny.

"Whatta ya say girls one more mission?"

Half pint barked, Jake smiled and nodded his head as he sat back waiting for his delivery. Jake was awakened by the feel of half pint's cold wet nose touching the back of his neck, as goosebumps covered both of Jake's arms he quickly sat up knocking the pizza box that was by his feet to the floor. "Holy shit that was cold." He said as he was wiping the crust from his eyes. "Ahh shit, damn it." He said now looking down at his feet, trying to wipe the marinara sauce from his sock. After about ten seconds of wiping Jake threw his hand up, took his socks off and threw both his socks and the pizza box into the trash can in his kitchen. Looking again at his phone and rereading the message from Murphy he took half pint and tiny for a walk, then went for his daily two mile run before taking a shower, getting dressed and making his way back to Murphy's house.

Chapter 23

I got up earlier than usual so I could shower, get dressed, and put some coffee on, I told everyone to be here at 8 o'clock. But I figured to get everything started in case anyone showed up early. And I was right, the doorbell rang at 7:45 looking through the peephole I saw Jake. "Good morning, your early."

"Yeah I got up and couldn't go back to sleep, I didn't wake you did I?"

"Oh no no I've been up but you look like shit are you OK?"

"Yeah rough night but I'm fine."

"Hell I've been there before, staying up late thinking about a case."

"Yeah something like that, so what's this break you found?"

Not saying another word I handed Jake the paper, as he in folded it he scrunched his eyebrows. "This is Arabic!"

"Yeah I know that's the problem we don't know what it says, I guess we could always Google it."

"Three tours to Iraq I learned a little Arabic, it says, come...."

"No shut up don't say it that's how you summon it we're not ready."

Jake stopped, folded the paper and put in his pocket.

When he did it was going on eight o'clock, and the doorbell started to ring. Steadman was the first one to show up right at eight o'clock on the nose, I always did like his punctuality within a few minutes the others showed up all within a few minutes apart. After everyone had arrived they congregated in the living room, with their cups of coffee and talking about whatever events occurred last night. After a few moments Jake came in from the kitchen, no coffee just the hand written note that would summon the demon. "OK everyone listen up, I think I know exactly how we are going to kill this damn thing." Jake announced looking a bit annoyed. The room grew quiet, so quiet you could literally hear a pin drop as all eyes fell on Jake. Then he continued. "There is an abandoned warehouse that I know of in Denver, its about twenty miles away from anything in any direction." "So did you just go looking for warehouses last night or what?" Julio sneered whilst taking a sip of his

coffee.

Jake unfazed by the comment continued. "No, when I first got out of the Marines I worked as a

security guard before becoming a police officer, it was one of the buildings I used to guard when it

was under construction. Anyway long story short the company ran out of money and its been sitting

there ever since." "Your sure its still abandoned?" Asked Steadman. "Yes positive, I still go out there

to let my dogs run around off of their leashes I was just down there a couple of days before Nancy

was killed." Danielle stood up and placed her coffee on the edge of the counter behind her, then

clapped her hands together. "OK so what are we waiting for, tell us the plan and let's go get this

damn thing." "I don't think its going to be that easy Danielle." I said to her from the kitchen, pouring

my second cup of coffee. "Well damn it Nancy was my friend, and this son of a bitch has already

killed way to many people." Jake raised his hands trying to calm Danielle down before speaking

again. "I know she was my friend too Danielle, and yes Murphy it is that easy."

I didn't say anything in response, I didn't have to I simply nodded my head while Steadman did his

famous "The Rock" eyebrow raise. "Come again, and how is that?" Steadman asked. "The I shape

ambush that we were talking about will work perfectly, I mean think about it when you are all in

position I will summon it. When I do it has to show up relatively close if he is going to try and kill me,

that should give at lest two of you a clear shot to take this thing down." "So your just going to

volunteer yourself just like that?" Asked Emma. "Well yeah I mean I am the only one that can speak

fluent Arabic, besides everyone else has families, loved ones, and social lives, all I have is my dogs."

Placing my hand on Jake's shoulder I asked him. "Are you sure about this, I mean have you thought it

through completely?" Jake had no hesitation in his response. "Yes as far as I'm concerned all my

family died in Iraq, so if the damn thing kills me the sooner I can see my brothers." "Jake I lost

peopl......" Jake instantly cut Steadman off. "Look Quincy my mind is made up, deal with it or I'll do it

myself." I then took a deep breath and as I exhaled I told him with a slight laugh. "Well if your that

sure, and there's no changing your mind." There's not." Jake snapped back abruptly. "Hell sounds

good when do we kill this damn thing?" Julio asked while he rested his head in one hand looking

down at the floor. Tonight, hell maybe we can kill this thing and still manage to keep our jobs." Jake

said back, sounding as sarcastic as possible. "Tonight?" Steadman said in response. Jake looked across the room quickly gathering his thoughts, then he locked eyes with Steadman. "Yes tonight, we

have the weapons, we have the ammo, and quite frankly I want to get this done before anyone gets

cold feet, myself included." Again silence this time for several minutes before Jake let out a long sigh,

before breaking the silence. "Well I'm going to get out of here, let's meet around 8o'clock providing

that's OK with you Scott?" I nodded still not saying anything. "What the hell are we supposed to do

until then?" Julio asked looking belittled. Jake shrugged. "Whatever you want, I'm going to find

someone to look after my dogs you know just in case." "In case of what?" Jake's eyes lowered, while

looking at the ground he spoke so softly it was almost a whisper. "In case it takes longer then we

think." Emma didn't say anything, none of us did we all knew what Jake meant. The thing is, is he

was right we all needed to think about what if this thing got us too. Again more silence, then without

saying a word Jake nodded and walked out the door. The rest of us stayed and pondered everything

that was said everyone except Danielle, she walked out the door a couple of seconds after Jake. She

watched as Jake did his inspection, Danielle wanted to approach him and say something. But what,

what could she say that would make a difference, what could she say that could bring closure to not

just him but all of them. As she stood in the driveway silent and motionless, she watched the

inspection, she watched him get into the car put his seat belt on, and as Jake pulled away they made

eye contact. Jake putting his car into gear gave Danielle a wink, pointed at her then drove away.

Danielle smiled and rolled her eyes, and instead of coming back into the house she too got in her car

and drove off.

Chapter 24

Rather than meet at Scott's house like we agreed, I got the address from Jake and punched it into my

GPS. When I got there I was a little early, a habit I picked up from the Air Force. But it was just like

Jake said, a run down warehouse pretty much in the middle of no where. I parked my car on the

south side of the building so the others could see my car as soon as they pulled up. Shifting my car

into park I let out a deep breath, turned my car off and got out. As I leaned against my car I took

another deep breath trying to mentally prepare myself for what I thought was going to happen here

tonight. Looking around there wasn't a single street light, just darkness. The air was cool, crisp and

was quiet not a sound not even from animals no crickets, no dogs barking nothing. It was to quiet,

quiet enough I swear you could feel the darkness and taste death in the air, and quite frankly it scared

the shit out of me. Trying to compose myself I began to pace back and forth along side my car

occasionally scuffing my feet, allowing a small dust trail to follow behind me. My nerves were just

about under control when I saw the first set of headlights appear. It was Murphy, "thank God." I

whispered to my self, then raised my hand in the air. Murphy flashed his spot light three times

blinding me each time, as he parked his car next to mine and got out. "You ass." I told him. Murphy

said nothing, he just grinned and stood beside me. "You look a little on edge." He said to me. "Yeah

no shit aren't you?" I said with a laugh. We stood there and bantered back and forth occasionally

pacing along side our vehicles for about ten minutes or so when we saw another set of headlights

appear from the distance, it was Jake, now I was really starting to get nervous now that the one who

was fluent in Arabic was here and able to summon the creature. Jake came in fast and stopped

abruptly causing a massive cloud of dust that seemed to engulf his car as he stopped, he turned his

car off as well as his headlights. Getting out of his car he laughed. "What the hell are you two doing

out here in the dark?" Murphy and I exchanged a quick glance before I spoke up. "Um excuse me?"

Another laugh followed. "Yeah I forgot to mention they never cut power to the place, so you could

have just turned the lights on." Murphy looked a cross between confused and pissed. "So this place still has electricity?" "Yeah I don't know why they never cut it but it still has power." Murphy and I

exchanged another quick glance, Murphy then rolled his eyes then the three of us began walking

toward the warehouses entrance. It was a large warehouse with a single dock door, and a single front

door and nothing else not even windows. As we were almost to the front entrance we could hear the

sound of another engine, the three of us stopped and turned to see another set of headlights, I

motioned for whoever was coming to follow. Walking into the warehouse it seemed colder then

outside, Jake quickly found the light switches and turned them all on. As the lights were warming up

they glowed white with a purplish hue around the edges of the bulb, I let out a sigh in doing so you

could see my breath leave my body and dissipate in the air. Also at that time Danielle and Julio

walked in, with their hands in their pockets. It seemed to be getting colder by the minute, of maybe it

was just me either way everyone was here now. "So were all finally here let's kill this fucker and get

this over with." I said sarcastically. Jake looked at and placed his hand on my shoulder. "Calm down

Steadman we will get him." Jake assured me. I smirked and nodded my head, then I looked around

the large empty warehouse and then at everyone that was there. "OK lets do this I said, with my

hands down by my side and shaking them trying to shake my nerves off. Jake looked around the

warehouse nervously, I could tell he wasn't trying to show it even though it was quite obvious.

"Alright fuck it let's do this." He said. Danielle grabbed his hand. "Should we pray or something?" She

asked. "No I'm fine I just want to get it done and over with." Regardless we still held hands and then

Jake cleared his throat and began. "Tati min baeidat tati min qurb jalb Shay-tan alzili huna yrja bsret

antakun sarieatan tadmir aedayiyin yrja an takun sarieatan." At that moment the lights seemed to

dim, as the single front door swung open and a thick black fog rushed in and quickly filled the room, it

then made its way to the center of the room and began swirling rapidly. While all this was going on

Julio unzipped the duffle bag he had brought in from his car, Julio pulled out an ar15, racked a round

in the chamber. Then quickly passed it to his right Danielle too pulled out and loaded a weapon, and

the process repeated until everyone had a rifle of some sort. It all happened so fast, the swirling

lasted only a couple of seconds and then it formed the shape of a human but looked nothing like one.

As the fog cleared it revealed a human like figure, in a hooded cloak that seemed to be made entirely

of the fog that came in and yet thick enough to conceal its entire body. Looking at the face I could see

the pale white face, only decaying a little around the jaw area, my guess was the more it fed the more it regenerated but I was to much in shock to say anything. As the creature stood before us he looked

almost as if he were confuses but only for a moment and as he looked he paused as it gazed upon

Danielle. It didn't say anything it just stared, first Danielle then to me, then it stopped at Jake and

began to walk towards him, and then paused again looking as if he recognized him from somewhere.

The creature slowly stepped closer to Jake, the lights seemed to have no effect on him at all. Then

another step in Jake's direction, Jake raised his rifle, aiming it center mass on the creatures chest. The

creature stopped, tilting its head slightly to the right, as if it were trying to assess its situation. Then it

went to take another step, Jake opened fire shooting three rounds. "Bang, Bang, Bang." But it was to

late, the creature turned back into the thick black fog at exactly the same time the first round was

fired. All three rounds went straight through the fog, where Julio was standing. The first round struck

him in the chest, the second in his head just above his right eye killing him instantly, as the third

ricocheted off the wall behind him. Before any of us could begin to grasp what happened, the

creature re formed this time standing only a few inches from Jake. Jake went to raise his rifle again,

the creature grabbed the barrel with one hand and pulled Jake toward him while he plunged his other

hand into Jake's stomach. We watched in horror, as the creature tossed Jake's rifle to the ground.

Now with one hand inside Jake's stomach, he wrapped his other hand around his throat and lifted

him off the ground. The creature turned to look at the rest of us, he then pulled his hand out of Jake's

stomach removing his intestines. The creature pulled them out wrapping them around Jake's neck,

then he began to float with Jake until reaching the ceiling. He then hung Jake from a light, and then

turned back into fog. Then vanished, Danielle Murphy and I were in shock we didn't move. "What

the Fuck just happened?" Danielle asked. Neither Murphy or I responded, I mean what could we say

we had a plan that went to shit. From start to finish we lost two people in less then ten minutes. I

looked to where Julio was standing, now laying in a small pool of blood his face caved in from the

bullet and parts brain matter and pieces of around the exit wound. I then looked at Murphy he to

was staring and Julio, then I looked to Danielle her eyes were fixed on Jake. Jake hung gentle

swinging back and forth with the occasional drip of blood, dripping from the end of his boot to the

warehouse floor.

Chapter 25

Looking at the horror that was bestowed upon us, I violently shook my head trying to snap out of the shock. Also I could feel the wind slowly picked up from a gentle breeze to slightly stronger with periods of gusts, not uncommon unless your inside a building. I ran over and grabbed Danielle's hand and shoved Quincy. "Come on you two we need to get the fuck out of here." My saying that got both their attention, the wind got even stronger as the black fog started to return, Danielle, Quincy and I ran toward the warehouse door. I got Danielle out the door and she got into my car, then Steadman, now it was my turn I ran out the door to my car. I stopped at the driver side door and looked back, at the doorway I saw the creature his face was now extremely decayed, his jaw barely hanging on. "Murphy what are you doing, let's fucking go." I heard Steadman yell from the passenger side. I quickly got in and started my car shifted it into drive and pushed the gas peddle to the floor. Now the wind was blowing so hard I could feel the car rocking side to side occasionally lifting two wheels off the ground, while I was driving and trying to see through the thick black fog that seemed to be everywhere I turned my driver side spotlight on. "Quincy get the other one." I yelled. Quincy frantically turned the passenger side spotlight on. "OK I got it, but what the hell?" "The light, the light it works it just isn't instant, it takes a minute.". That being said Quincy turned the passenger side spot light in facing us, I nodded and did the same with the driver side. As I drove I could see glimpses of the creatures face on the left and occasionally the right side as well periodically bumping the side of the car, trying to spin us. It was hard to drive with both the constant light in my eyes and the creature hitting the car but then it suddenly stopped. "What the hell Murph where did it go?" "I don't know bu......". Just then the glass shattered in the back seat, the fog rushed in and then out taking Danielle with it. "Steadman what the fuck just happened?" I asked trying desperately to evade the creature.

"It got her, it got Danielle." Steadman screamed tears now filling his eyes, as he just watched his crush get sucked out of a window. As I drive hitting bump after bump, and trying to maintain control of my car. The wind suddenly stopped, the banging against my car came to a cease, and the air began to clear. "What the fuck?"   "I don't know Quincy." I said shifting my car into park, and getting out I

drew my side arm from its holster, getting in the low ready position and began looking around my

car. Steadman got out right behind me, pistol drawn and in the high ready position. "Hey Murph

what happened to the L shape ambush?" "I don't know Quincy." "What happened to the whole

plan?" "God damn it Quincy I don't know."

We both made our way to the back of the car, his pistol high mine low, we were looking and waiting

for what ever would happen next. But nothing came nothing happened, it was quite, crickets began

to chirp, and an over all peace came over the area. Steadman and I started walking back towards the

driver and passenger side of my car. When I paused I wasn't the only one Steadman did too, and by

some weird coincidence we both looked up at the same time. "Murph what the fuc..." We both

dropped to the ground and rolled away from the car. As something slammed on the top of my car, as

we stood up we said nothing to one another we knew it was Danielle. "Son of a bitch." Steadman said

while dropping to his knees. I holstered my weapon and walked over to Steadman, I put one hand on

his shoulder and slowly used my other to try and take Steadman's pistol from him. He was reluctant

at first, but with his tears starting to dry on his face he looked up nodded his head and let me have his

weapon until he could finish composing himself. I stood there with Steadman for the next fifteen

minutes with my hand on his shoulder, not saying anything just giving him an occasional pat or two on

his shoulder. Then he reached up and grabbed my hand. "Hey Murph." He said. "Yeah Quincy."

"Where's my gun?" I took my hand off his shoulder, and handed him back his gun. He gave me

another head nod, then placed his gun back in its holster and started walking back towards the

warehouse. "Steadman what are you doing, don't forget we have to call all of this in." "No Murph I

ain't calling in shit, I'm going home." "Steadman you can't ju..." "Yes I can Murphy and I'm going to,

this whole damn case just got ripped apart. We have no more leads, no witnesses, no evidence at lest

none we can use, and even if we did no one in their right mind would believe it anyway. Now we just

lost Julio, Jake, and Danielle, we have nothing Murphy so I'm going to get in my car and I'm going the

fuck home if you want to report me then fine." I could not believe what Steadman just said, we have

worked together for years and I had never seen this side of him ever. I watched in amazement as he

walked back to his car slamming the door as he got in, he started it and sped off leaving me there.

Chapter 26

Emma knew Scott was going to be out late tonight, but she still wanted it everything just right for when he got home. She had food ready for him in the microwave, the house was spotless, the clothes were washed, she even put fresh sheets on the bed. Now she decided it was time for her to unwind until Murphy came home. "He deserves it." She thought, after all he had been working so hard on trying to stop this monster. She poured herself a glass of Château Lafite 1865 an anniversary gift she was just getting around to. She sat down on the couch, kicked her feet up and turned the on the television. Some detective show about catching serial killers was on she watched for about an hour, finding her self pointing out all of the mistakes that they made on TV much like Murphy does when he watches these programs. Then poured another glass of Château, turning off the television, all the lights, and walking into the bedroom. Striping along the way leaving a trail of close from the living room into the bedroom, once in the bedroom she set her glass of wine on her nightstand removed her panties and pulled back the freshly made silk sheets. Emma climbed into bed the sheets cool and gave her goosebumps as she nestled down and pulled the sheet back over her body Another sip of wine and thinking to herself that this was going to be a very special night indeed, she finished her wine and began to doze off to sleep. As she slept awaiting Scott's return she kept waking up periodically checking the time, using the restroom, and checking to make sure the alarm on the house was set. Finally she fell into a deep sleep but still would toss and turn, from time of time then Emma's body became still after a moment or two. As she slept the house became darker, and a light breeze blew through the house and the black fog came in from under the front door. Shay-tan Alzili now stood at the front door of Murphy's house, and as he steps out from the shadows an approaches Emma. He stops but only for a moment, he can't help thinking that no one will stop him. As he now stands at the end of the bed, he grins a brief smile slightly revealing his razor sharp teeth stained with a dark yellowish tint. He reaches his partly decaying hands up and removed the black hood from his head. His face was pale like the whiteness of the moon and covered in scars, in some places chunks of flesh missing showing parts of his skull. He slowly crept closer and removed the black silk sheet revealing her naked body, he let's out another smile. "They are all the same." He thought. As he walked up ever so gently dragging his index finger up the right side of her body first her started at the ankle, then to her thigh, to her breast, until finally he reaches her throat. The creature gently wrapped his fingers around Emma's throat and leans forward. "Thiss is what happens when your husband tries to hunt me, thiss was not meant for you but he must learn." He whispered. His hand then tightly squeezed her throat. "This is it." He thought. As Emma awoke her eyes filled with terror. "Your to late no amount of light can save you now." As he tightens his grip digging his monstrous claws deep into Emma's neck and tore it out, her head bounced as it hit the floor rolling slightly under the bed. Shay-tan Alzili then began to eat Emma's esophagus, enjoying every bite, every second of his meal because was uncertain the next time he would be able to feed. He also knew that no one would ever try to purposely summon him again, after consuming his meal he leaves Emma's lifeless body, then slowly slipped back into the shadow from which he came and disappeared.

Chapter 27

After calling in what happened at the warehouse Murphy knew he would spend hours with the other

detectives when they arrived on scene, another couple hours doing the paperwork. However

surprisingly the first person to arrive was Steadman, he pulled in just as fast as he left. Murphy was

bewildered at what was happening, Steadman now slamming on his breaks and throwing his car into

park so fast and so violently that the entire car jerked a couple of times as he leapt out leaving the

door open. "What the fuck Murph you can't answer your phone?" Murphy scowled his eyes, now

even more confused. "What it didn't ring." "Murph fox and I have been trying to call you for almost

an hour now, you need to come with me." "Steadman I can't what abou..." "Fuck the scene Scott get

in the damn car, its not over I don't have time to explain just get and let's fucking go." Steadman

yelled now grabbing Murphy by his arms and began trying to force him into the car. "Shit Quincy I'm

coming." Murphy said getting in the passenger seat, Steadman slammed the door almost hitting

Murphy's shoulder while doing so, Steadman then ran to the driver side jumping in while at the same

time closing the door and shifting into drive all in one smooth motion. Steadman then sped off his

tires spun as he drove off kicking up a few loose rocks and leaving trail of dust behind the car.

Speeding back towards the interstate Steadman kept mumbling to himself not really talking, I leaned

over and took a look at the speedometer. "95, OK Quincy level with me what the hell is going on?"

Not a word from Steadman he just glanced over at me then back to the road and sped up even more.

I knew it must be something important for him to have his emergency lights flashing and to go

through every red light and stop sign. I really didn't pay it much attention, its not the first time we

have had to race from call to call. The only thing that was bothering me was him not talking, he

always talks, the hard part is getting him to shut up. Something had to be wrong, I mean aside from

the warehouse full of dead off duty police officers, but I couldn't put my finger on it. After about an

hour of Steadman's insane driving and my occasional staring off into space, contemplating the events

and how it all unfolded tonight. As i snapped myself back into reality, I noticed that Steadman just turned onto Colorado blvd. "Quincy where are you taking me?" I asked. He said nothing, he just kept driving I didn't really start insisting until I saw he turned on Mexico. "Steadman what the hell I live on this street." "I know." He said. Then he was quite again, after two or three blocks I could see the blue lights flashing.

Chapter 28

Steadman threw the car into park and got out, Murphy quickly followed behind him, captain Fox was there and met them before they got to the police tape. "Steadman what the hell took so long, and when I said to take him somewhere I did not mean hear." "This is my house, this is my house Drew what the hell happened?" Captain Fox lowered his eyes and took a deep breath, then looked back at Murphy. Fox gently grabbed Murphy by his shoulders. "Murph I'm so sorry, its Emma.." Murphy shook his shoulders free from fox and pushed him away. "What the hell do you mean." "Murph I sorry." Fox repeated. Murphy's eyes widened as a lump in his throat began to form while he started walking towards his house. Murphy now standing at his front door, his palms were sweating, his heart pounding as he reached for the door knob. Murphy grasped the door knob turned it and walked in, now standing at the entrance of his house he looked around. He looked at the other police officers, he looked at the detectives that were taking pictures in his living room. But what caught his eye was the flash from a camera from inside his bedroom. As he pushed past the detectives and other officers, he walked into his bedroom. Murphy immediately felt weak as if he were going to pass out, his legs felt like the were going to give out. In order to keep from collapsing he fell onto his dresser and held on, while trying to fight back the overwhelming urge to vomit. Murphy stood there leaning against the dresser looking at the body covered in a white sheet, know one had to say anything he knew it was Emma. With his legs shaking he took a step away from the dresser and towards the body, his first step and he almost collapsed, trying desperately to compose himself he managed to leave the dresser and approach the body. Just as Murphy was standing next to Emma's body his legs gave out and Murphy collapsed, his hands where shaking uncontrollably as he reached up and removed the sheet revealing Emma. As Murphy gazed at his lifeless Emma, he began to scream while weeping at the same time. "Not me, not my house, not my Emma." He repeated to himself. Murphy sat on the floor now holding his wife's headless body with one hand and desperately trying to reattach her head with the other. Murphy held Emma's head and body in his arms and rocked back and forth, he stopped when he felt Steadman touch him on his shoulder. "All right

everyone clear out, let's give him a minute for fucks sake." Shouted Steadman. The room quickly

emptied, and as it did Fox walked up to Steadman, now standing next to him he looked around the

room. "Quincy this is still a crime scene." Steadman nodded his head in agreement. "Yup and did

you know I don't care, the man just lost his wife." Fox didn't say anything else instead he held the

door for Steadman, then closed it on his way out. Fox looked at Steadman. "What the hell happened

Quincy, thought you said it was under control, that you could kill the damn thing." "Yes captain you

can kill it but you don't understand, you didn't see the way this thing can move, the speed it can

change form, I've never seen something move so fast." "So now what Quincy, any ideas because I'm

open to anything." Steadman and Fox said nothing both of them were lost in thought, so much so

that they didn't notice Murphy had exited the room and was standing behind both of them. "Lets

blow the bitch up!" Murphy said. Steadman almost jumped out of his skin. "Jesus Christ Scott I

didn't hear you come out are you trying to give me a heart attack." Fox jumped to and the laughed at

Quincy for his reaction. "Sorry Steadman not trying to." Fox raised an eyebrow. "Blow it up Scott?"

Asked Fox. "Yes Drew blow it up, we underestimated this thing a mistake I will not make again.

Steadman looked puzzled. "How do propose we do that Scott, you saw how fast it moves the way it

moves." "Yeah Steadman I know, but what if we built a bomb, summon him again and as soon as he

shows up we detonate." Steadman ran his hand over his head. "Its worth a shot, I mean why not."

Fox threw his hands up. "Are you two seriously going after this thing again, are you both nuts.?" Fox

stormed off mumbling and cursing out the front door slamming it shut, hard enough it shook the

pictures that hung on the wall of the foyer. Steadman let out a laugh. "You know we are probably

going fired for this Scott." "Its OK let's worry about not dying first then I'll worry about the job."

Nothing else was said, Steadman stood there with Murphy, as they watched the police officers

conduct their investigation. Watched as they took their notes and photographs, watched as the

corner loaded Emma's body and placed it in the ambulance. Watched as everyone left the house and

drove down the street, now with nobody but Steadman and Murphy left in the house. Steadman

clapped his hands three times. "Holy shit what a day, I don't know about you but I need a beer, come

on let's go." "Go, go where?" "Scott your not staying here tonight so lets go get hammered I'm

buying, then we catch an uber to my place then whenever we wake up then we will start figuring shit out." Murphy didn't say anything, he grabbed his coat and walked to Steadmans car. "You not going

to lock it?" Steadman yelled. "Screw it if someone really wants something let them have it."

Steadman shrugged his shoulders and closed the door, he and Murphy got in his car and drove off.

Chapter 29

I don't know what I was thinking getting into Steadman's car but with the night I had and then Emma

on top of everything I was really just going with the flow at this point. Steadman drove off from my

house and twenty minutes later we pulled up to the Royal Hilltop, it was a pretty nice bar from what I

could tell. Steadman and I sat down and waited for the bartender, she was around Steadmans age,

she stood about 5'1" if she was lucky, with bright red hair that was cut unusually short for my taste.

Steadman found her very attractive, as she walked her eye caught Steadman she leaned over resting

her for arms on the bar showing off her cleavage. "Hi I'm Brittany, what can I get you boys?" "Let's

start with two triples of Johnny red, and a bucket of Coors light." "You got it sweety." She said while

gently touching Steadman's hand. I couldn't help but roll my eyes. As Brittany laid the shot glasses

down and poured the Scotch, I took my glass took a small sip and as the burning sensation warmed

my chest I swirled my glass watching the liquid rotate. Another small sip and I looked up at the

television behind the counter just above us, the Broncos were playing the patriots and thank god the

broncos were winning. I sat with a grin on my face watching the game, I was pleased to see the

broncos beating the patriots. That and I was trying my damnedest to take my mind off of the events

that took place tonight especially Emma. Looking over at Steadman as he continued to flirt with

Brittany, when he glanced over I raised my glass and finished my Scotch then reached into the ice

filled bucket picked up a beer and twisted the cap off. I placed the bottle to my lips as I was in mid sip

Brittany came over, she poured two more shots and put them in front of me then she poured two in

front of Steadman. "Those are on the house, you and your friend look like you need it." She said with

a playful smile looking at Steadman. "Do you two need some privacy?" I asked Steadman, not taking

my eyes off of the television. Steadman smile got a mile wide. "Naw its all good, come on let's play

some pool." Steadman and I must have played three or four games, the rest of the night was kind of

a blur. As the night went on it was shot after shot, beer after beer, story after story. Then the night

started to die down, last call was called and the bar lights brightened and the music stopped.

Everything was blurry and as much as I didn't want to admit it, after everything I think I needed the distraction and I think Steadman somehow knew that. We walked outside to wait for our uber driver, as the alcohol started taking effect I don't remember what our driver looked like I remembered closing my eyes and as the darkness faded to black I fell asleep.

Chapter 30

I woke up undressed in my bed, I have no idea how I got there all I know is my head was pounding, as I looked over at my night stand there was two Tylenol and a bottle of water. After taking the Tylenol I went to get out of my bed, Brittany was sleeping on the floor next to my bed. ' What the fuck ' I thought to myself. I stepped over Brittany as gently as I could walked down the hall and into my living room. Murphy was there sleeping on my couch. "Must have been one hell of a night." I said out loud to myself. I opened my refrigerator and took out a carton of orange juice, and a glass. "Can I have some too?" Brittany asked from behind me. Not missing a beat I pulled a second glass, and poured both of us a glass. "Look about last night." "Yeah about that, look you were in no condition to drive, that and not to mention your uber driver looked sketchy as hell. I mean can you say serial killer, so I got the keys to your car and drove you home." "OK but how did you know where I live?" "Um you told me, don't you remember anything?" I took a sip of my orange juice and shook my head. "Nope, what about us di...." No no no, nothing like that you might have been drunk as hell but still a gentleman, you didn't try any funny business."

"So you just go home with random strangers?" Murphy asked now stretching and sitting up from the couch. "Maybe I'm wrong, but I felt pretty safe taking to drunk cops home." I set my orange juice down. "Wait how did you know we were cops?" "Really detective Murphy both of you had your badges clipped to your belts, and when I asked for Quincy's ID he showed me his P.O.S.T. ID card. Come on everyone knew you two were cops last night, it's not like you two were being discrete about it." "Steadman she's kind of a smart ass." "I've noticed, and I think we will get along just fine." I told Murphy while winking at Brittany. Brittany blushed slightly and smiled. "Well I really should be going, but feel free to call me." She said writing her number in the palm of Steadmans hand. After Brittany left, Murphy and I had to make a coffee run to the dunkin donuts that was right around the corner. Rather than hitting the drive thru we decided to go inside and sit down, after we got our coffee Murphy cleared his throat, and sat down. Taking his glasses off and setting them on the table, he gave his eye a quick rub while letting out a groan. "What are we going to do?" He asked. "About what?" "Christ, everything Steadman, these past few months have gone to shit, and now with losing Emma I don't even know if I can do this anymore." "Do what, Murph what are you talking about you love this job." "What I mean Quincy is I have done this job for so long that I've gone numb to almost everything, hell Emma was literally the only reason I kept putting the damn badge on every day, and now that she's gone I'm asking myself. Do I really want to keep doing this, hell Quincy I'm old, to old to be chasing down criminals, or biblical creatures for that matter." Murphy took a sip of his coffee and then smiled. "But Quincy you, your still young you still have time to make an impact on lives, hell to do what Emma and I couldn't." "Oh yeah Murph and what's that." "Do I have to spell it out, go start a family, take a trip somewhere, enjoy what you have before it all slips away like it did to me." I said nothing, I couldn't, I was trying to carefully choose my words while slowly nodding my head up and down. "So Murph, look if you need to take a few days to figure everything out, trust me we will understand." Murphy put his glasses back on his face and looked around the room as if searching for the right words to say. Murphy lowered his eyes and let out a smirk. "You know what Steadman I think your right, I think I will take a few days off, and if you don't mind will you take me back to my place?, after all I need to make some phone calls to Emma's family, and I have a funeral to plan, you understand don't you?"

"Oh yeah absolutely." I told him. After that Murphy and I got up and left to take Murphy home, and that would give me the chance to toss things around in my mind. I knew if I told Murphy that I wanted to go after the creature again he would try and talk me out of it, so I thought it be best to keep my mouth shut. I watched as Murphy finished his coffee, staying quite and contemplating my next three moves much like a game of chess. First move take Murphy home. Second move go back to the warehouse. And third kill that damn demon, all I have to do is remember the mistakes that were made and try not to duplicate them. "Easier said then done." Murphy looked at me over his glasses.

"I'm sorry what?"

Oh shit I said that a loud, I smiled and started laughing. "Wait what oh nothing Murph I was just thinking out loud."

"Really, about what?" Murphy asked as he took his glasses back off placing them back on the table, as he looked at me he interlaced his fingers placed them in front of his face and raised his eyebrows. I smiled and tried to let out another laugh, however it came out as more of a choke rather than a laugh. "Umm nothing just thinking about some personal things." "Brittany?" "Uh yeah, yeah yeah, of course Brittany." After we finished I took Murphy home like I promised, as Murphy got out he paused and leaned into the passenger side window. "You sure you...." "Murph it's fine." I interrupted. Murphy stepped back, nodded his head. "See you around Murph." I said, as I drove off rolling the window up.

Chapter 31

After dropping Murphy off Steadman drove straight back to the warehouse, after arriving he decided to look around. He walked around the building and then went inside, standing in the doorway Steadman begun to vomit from the sight and the smell. "WHAT THE FUCK?" He yelled. As he looked around the room, and let the reality set. "Nobody came, this doesn't make sense I know Murph called it in." Steadman looked as Jake still hung, swinging from the ceiling, Julio still slumped over blood and brain matter still on the wall behind him. Then Steadman looked at the weapons still on the floor, and the bag that still had the grenades no one got time to use. Steadman bent down and picked up one of the ak-47s as well as two grenades, he then walked over to a nearby window adjacent to were Julio was and took a deep breath in trying to salvage some fresh air. He took a moment to look around at the calm nothingness, the silence, the cool gentle breeze that hit his face. He had to try and compose himself as best he could so he could deal with what was inside, and what he was about to attempt. Walking into the center of the room Steadman reached into his pocket and pulled a folded piece of paper and with his hands now starting to shake he unfolded it. Looking at the paper he felt a lump begin to grow in his throat. "Pull it together Steadman, its weak right now in the daylight its not as strong." He told himself. Steadman now holding the paper at face level he began the chant. "Tati min baeidat tati min qurb Jalb Shay-tan alzili huna yrja beret antakun sarieatan tadmir aedayiyin yrja an takun sarieatan."

After the chant was completed, the wind began to get stronger, and stronger almost to hurricane strength. The black mist quickly flooded into the warehouse, it began swirling rapidly just like before. The creature now stood before him, Steadman looked up at the creature. Letting go of the paper it slowly fell to the floor he and the creature both watched as it hit the floor, just as it did Steadman opened fire, firing several rounds four of five of witch hit the creature. The creature let out a demonic blood curtailing scream, his mouth opened showing the razor sharp teeth that had already killed so many. His jaw extended almost double its original length, his tongue came out past his chin, then he screamed once more and ran towards Steadman. Steadman too let out a scream and fired

more shots at the demon, non seemed to effect him now, and just like with Jake the demon plunged

its claws deep into Steadman's stomach. As they raised off the floor Steadman grabbed a hold of the

the demons arm as tightly as he could with one hand. As they got higher Steadman let go of the

demons arm and reached into his pocket and began to laugh, as he did blood oozed from the side of

his mouth. "You laugh in the face of death?" The creature asked. Steadman now begging to choke

on his own blood started to laugh harder, as he did the demon and started to descend. When

Steadman's feet touched the floor the creature jerked his head as he heard the sound of the grenade

pin hit the floor. "DIE MOTHER FUCKER!" Steadman screamed. Steadman pushed and held the

grenade to the demon's chest, as he did everything seemed to slow down. He thought about his

parents back home, about Jake, Emma, Julio, Danielle, he thought about Murphy and the advice he

tried to give him at the donut shop. But none of it mattered, not any more, as the grenade exploded

against the demon's chest shrapnel filled the demon's chest as well as Steadman's. The force of the

blast sent Steadman and the demon hurtling across the room, both of their bodies lay lifeless on

opposite sides of the room and just before Steadman took his last breath he felt at peace knowing it

was finally over.

Chapter 32

It had been two weeks after Emma and Steadman's funeral, they had only been a day a part and the eulogy from both services still rang loudly in Murphy's head. Murphy sitting in his lazy boy in the living room, slouching so low that his shoulders almost touched where his buttocks should sit, his buttocks hanging off the chair and his legs stretched out to almost the center of the living room. In his right hand Murphy held a picture of he and Steadman when Steadman got promoted to detective, in Murphy's left hand a half drunk bottle of Jack Daniels, and on the television, was he and Emma's wedding video. Murphy sat there holding both the picture and the bottle, while blankly staring at the ceiling.

"Knock, knock knock." Murphy groaned, as his front door opened. "So we just leave doors unlocked now Murph, that's not like you." Murphy lifted his head just enough to see captain Fox, then let out another groan. "So Murphy I brought you some food and I though.......Jesus Christ Murph you look like shit." "Grrr thanks for noticing, now what do you want?"

"Umm I told you I stopped by to check on you, and make sure you were eating and I'm glad I did when was the last time you ate, or did anything?" "Who fucking cares I still have another week of vacation time." "Ok Murph get up, get dressed, let's go." "Argh what the hell are you talking about Drew I'm not going anywhere, the only thing I'm going to do is polish this bottle of Tennessee's finest and then I'm gonna get another. Instead of lather, rinse, repeat. It's drink, drunk, repeat. Now if you'll excuse me I know I have another bottle in the garage. Murphy finally got out of his lazy boy and stumbled to his feet, after managing to get his balance he looked at Fox who was still holding a couple bags of groceries. Murphy then tossed the picture of he and Steadman, on to the chair and holding one finger up. "Just a sec Drew." Murphy said, as he started chugging the rest of the bottle. "Goddamnit Murph." Captain Fox yelled, dropping the bags on the floor, Fox ran over and slapped the bottle from Murphy's hand knocking it to the ground, the bottle shattered as soon as it hit the floor, glass and liquor now lay in front of the living room window. Murphy punched captain Fox as soon as the bottle hit the floor, Fox holding his jaw. "Murph what the hell." " Fuck you Fox, you don't have a clue what it's like, your wife is still alive, you were able to have kids, I lost everything the second you put me on this fucking case. "

"Is that what you think happened Murphy, you think I wanted any of this to happen, no we had a serial killer and I put my two best detectives on the case because I knew it would get done, and get done right. I had no clue we were going to go up against some biblical fucking death dealer." Murphy began to pace the floor rapidly mumbling to himself, then walked into the kitchen. "I want you out." He said to Fox. "Murphy." Murphy opened the drawer next to the sink. "Goddamnit Fox I said get the fuck out of my house." Murphy yelled pulling out a p90 ruger and pointing at Fox.

"Holy shit Murph ok just calm down I'm gonna go, nice gun is it new you kno..." "Just go." Murphy said calmly. "Ok, ok you got it buddy just call me if you need anything." Fox backed away slowly and left Murphy at home with his gun, liquor , and thoughts. He knew it was a bad idea, but at the same time he thought that he would probably act the same way if he were in those shoes. "He'll be fine." he said to himself as he drove off. Murphy as soon as the door closed began to cry, dropping to his knees in the kitchen he set the gun on the floor and for several minutes he wept. He had lost everything and now he just pointed a loaded weapon at not only his boss but his friend for over twenty years. When Murphy finally stopped crying, he picked up his gun and got up off the floor, holding the gun tightly in his right hand he walked to the garage opened the door and walked out to retrieve the bottle of Jack Daniels he had stashed away. He knew Emma didn't like him drinking hard liquor, but he always kept some in the garage. After he got his other bottle he went back into the living room and sat back in his lazy boy. Murphy opened the bottle and drank half the bottle in one sip. "Ahh that's better." He said as he looked at the broken bottle across the room, Murphy groaned and adjusted himself reaching behind him pulling out the picture that he had tossed earlier. Murphy finished the rest of the bottle with his next sip, he leaned back in the chair and dropped the bottle to the floor. After a few minutes he could feel the alcohol taking effect, his vision became blurry, and even tho he was sitting still he felt the room starting to sway. Memories flooded Murphy's head everything from when he first met Emma, to where he was now and everything in between. Murphy felt overwhelmed and threw the picture against the window cracking the glass before falling next to the broken bottle of Jack. Murphy then leaned back in his chair picked up the remote control that was setting on the arm rest he restarted he and Emma's wedding video and began to cry once again.

By now Murphy was feeling the full force of the alcohol, his head began rocking back and forth, he also had double vision and room went from swaying to feeling like he was in a roller coaster. Murphy looked around the room as the alcoholic depression deeply set in he looked down and realized that he was still holding his gun in his hand. With his hand still tightly grasped around the gun, he looked up at the television, at the final part of him finishing his vows to Emma. At that moment Murphy completely lost all rational thought, he jumped up out of the chair and shot one round through the television. Murphy now in a drunken rage stuffed the gun into his pants and began destroying his house. He ripped the television from the entertainment center and threw it across the room, he began punching holes into the walls, and knocking pictures off the wall. Finally after destroying the living room and completely exhausting himself he fell to the floor once again. Breathing heavily Murphy pulled the gun from his waist and placed it under his chin. "I'm so sorry Emma." Murphy said. And then pulled the trigger, unfortunately death was not instant. As the blood poured out of his head, mouth and nose, he began choking on the blood that seeped down into his lungs. As Murphy's filled with blood and he started fading in and out of consciousness he saw a dark outline now walking towards him, as it got closer he realized that it was Emma. But how Murphy wondered as Emma started to reach out to him, Murphy smiled as Emma got closer her body now outlined in a whitish glow. Murphy gasped his last breath and closed his eyes, the blood continued to drain from his wounds, and as his body went limp Murphy passed away.

ONE WEEK LATER

Chapter 33

Captain Fox rode in the back of the motorcade only two cars behind the Hurst and on this chilly and

rainy morning, as Fox watched the overpasses with the fire trucks and American flags draped over

them. He couldn't help but think that it was all his fault, thinking what if he had not pushed Murphy

so hard, or what if he had came back would it have changed anything. At this point it really didn't

matter the only thing that mattered now is he had to try and focus on not falling apart while he had

to give yet another eulogy, when he had given so many over the years and now it was the second one

he had to do for a personal friend. As the rain set in and started to get heavier the motorcade pulled

into the cemetery, people in the hundreds attended and as they vacated their vehicles. As everyone

found and took their seats, Fox walked onto the stage looking at all the attendees all dressed in black

and most with matching black umbrellas. Fox took a deep breath and exhaled as he did you could

see his breath fill the air as he stood in front of the microphone, clearing his throat he began the

eulogy. It took roughly an hour and a half with Fox occasionally tearing up and choking on his words,

but it was finally over everyone paid their final respects to Murphy and left. Of course a few people

lingered to banter about how he would be missed and on how he was such a great guy. But not Fox,

Fox was just ready to get the hell out of there and as swiftly and politely as possible left the funeral,

and got into his car. Knowing damn well his day was just beginning so sitting in his car he composed

himself, and decided to drive to the office. As he drove he couldn't help but reminisce about

Murphy,Steadmen,and the whole damn case leading up to the funerals. Fox was so distracted he

got to his office faster than he anticipated,never the less he made it to the office unlocked the door

and walked in. Not bothering to turn the lights on he walked to his desk, sitting down buried his

face in his hands and began to cry again. "Murphy you motherfucker I didn't see this coming, you

were always such a fighter." Fox began to compose himself and turned on his desk light, he leaned

back in his chair kicked his feet on the desk and grabbed the case file and opened it. With a heavy

sigh began working on cases putting his signature where it was needed,and as he did his desk lamp flickered.   Fox chuckled and tapped his lamp.   " come on don't you die on me too."   As the flickering stopped he began to sign more papers, then the light flickered again and turned off then back on.   When the light came back on the little girl was standing on the other side of his desk, her skin still pale her hair covered her face, her body gently shaking as she slowly cocked her head to the side. "HOLY SHIT!" Shouted Fox.   The girl softly started to whisper.   "Tati min baeidat tati min qurb Jalb Shaytan Alzili huna yrja beret antakun sarieatan tadmir aedayiyin yrja an takun sarieatan."   Fox now frozen both in fear and disbelief, watching as the dark mist starts coming in from under the door and began taking his demonic form,and as it was taking form it muttered "ana shaytan alzili."   then the girl straightened her head back up right,her hair uncovered her face showing her blood shot eyes and blue lips.   The girl smiled showing her decaying teeth then the desk light turned off.

www.ingramcontent.com/pod-product-compliance
Lightning Source LLC
Chambersburg PA
CBHW030528260626
47157CB00005B/1936